"The setting of this gem of a novella is deftly wrought and alluringly atmospheric. With the smoke of climate disasters billowing on the horizon, the distressed and angsty hotel rooms, unkempt apartments, and punk bars, this story is about the power that time holds over our transient lives. The frantic pursuit of bionic memory and immortality, DeBellis shows us, will not elevate humanity. Only art, electric and ephemeral—only nature, imperiled and persistent—only life, grievously and marvelously short—can do that."

— M. C. BENNER DIXON, AUTHOR OF
THE HEIGHT OF LAND

METHUSELAH

METHUSELAH

AMY DEBELLIS

Methuselah

Copyright © 2026 by Amy DeBellis

Cover by Amy DeBellis

First edition: 2026

Printed in the United States of America.

No part of this book was assisted by, generated by, or developed with AI.

This is a work of fiction. Unless otherwise indicated, all the names, characters, businesses, places, events, and incidents in this book are either the product of the author's imagination or used in a fictitious manner. Any resemblance to actual persons, living or dead, or actual events is purely coincidental.

No part of this book may be reproduced in any form or by any electronic or mechanical means, including information storage and retrieval systems, without written permission from the author, except for the use of brief quotations in a book review.

For Wilma, my grandmother

Some girl a hundred years ago once lived as I do.
And she is dead. I am the present, but I know I, too,
will pass. The high moment, the burning flash,
come and are gone, continuous quicksand.

- Sylvia Plath

My yesterdays walk with me. They keep step, they
are gray faces that peer over my shoulder.

- William Golding

CHAPTER ONE

BARSTOW, CALIFORNIA, 2014

Tessa's father was fond of reminding her that she was the first person in her family not to go to college since her great-grandparents. "Well, makes sense," she would reply. "That's why they're great and I'm not." It didn't make sense, but she would laugh anyway, her stoned, stupid-sounding laugh, as her father grew more and more disapproving on the other end of the phone.

They had to get in contact mostly by phone these days, because Tessa hadn't been home in months. Being on the road did that to you. Since dipping politely out of the college track, she'd been touring with her doom metal band, Pestilential Harbor, for nearly a year. Only a small portion of that had actually fit the technical definition of touring—booking shows and playing to live audiences that numbered between ten and two hundred—but she liked to tell people they had been touring for a year, because it elicited a certain level of respect. But the reality of Pestilential Harbor being on the road was a lot more grueling and a lot less glamorous than most people thought.

"Pestilential Harbor? What is that, a disease?" Tessa's

father had asked her when she'd first told him about it. "A lesser demon? A hotel that nobody ever comes back from?"

"No," she'd said, proud at his discomfiture. "It's a doom metal band. *My* doom metal band. And it's going to be a success. It won't turn into a demon—probably."

"See that it doesn't."

Now, nearly a year later, she tried to tell him as little as possible. Yes, they'd been on the road for eleven months, snaking from San Jose to Fresno to San Bernardino and then back up north to Sacramento and Quincy and Redding, and then down to Sacramento again, then Fresno, then Barstow. Yes, they'd been working on their music. No, they hadn't been booking as many venues as they'd wanted to. Yes, they were mainly coasting on the money from Nico the bassist and his parents, who for some reason still gave him an allowance, despite him being the oldest of all of them.

Yes, they had no future.

Every day they would smoke weed and brainstorm and work, or attempt to work, on their music. Every night they would have breakdowns. One night it would be Emrys the drummer, and the next night it was Zac the rhythm guitarist. They were polite; they took turns.

Tonight it was Nico's turn. It was the middle of July, the air tasting like leaves and moss and things pulled up from the darkness underground. They were staying in a motel right now, just to get out of the RV. Things were hardly less cramped in the motel: it was Tessa and Alistair in one room, and Zac, Nico, and Emrys in another. Tonight they were all gathered in Tessa and Alistair's room, and despite the open window, the space quickly filled with the fecund, skunky odor of pot. Whenever one of them cracked a beer lid a new layer of scent would form on top: yeast, ammonia, the tang of vinegar. Every once in a while, a light would sweep by the window and throw a ghostly cast over their faces. Tessa found herself unable to stop glancing at Alistair whenever this happened, at what was illuminated there: his crooked nose, his sweep of dark hair above pale brown, almost ochre-colored eyes.

"We would've gone under long ago if it wasn't for me," said Nico, staring into the depths of his can of beer. "I'm the only thing keeping us afloat. It's pathetic."

"Yeah, we know, Nico." Zac prepared to take another pull on his joint. Thick dark hair, so deep brown it was almost black, nearly obscured his eyes. "You've bragged enough."

Zac was the band member Tessa knew the least. She'd known Nico and Emrys since high school, had gleefully boycotted prom and pretty much every other non-mandatory school event (and some mandatory ones) with them and her other friends. As a fledgling, the band had consisted only of the three of them, but then Zac and Alistair joined a few months later, sauntering in thanks to one of Nico's Craigslist ads.

"Who's bragging?" Nico slammed his beer down on the rug, a gesture that did not produce the sound he'd probably hoped for (the rug was very soft, almost squishy). "How is it bragging to have a band that literally only exists because of my freakin' allowance? Not because of talent, or ambition, but because of my mommy and daddy?"

Zac, with the smoke still in his lungs, just looked at him. Finally he exhaled, and coughed spastically. "Mostly mommy," he choked out.

Nico drained the rest of his beer and threw the empty can at him. It bounced off his knee.

Tessa got up to open the window further. It creaked

hideously as she dragged it down, squealing like a mouse being stepped on. The still-warm July air seeped in, and she felt it collect on her skin, bits of dirt attaching themselves to her forehead and cheeks and sweaty armpits. There seemed to be no vegetation outside besides scrubby grass and palm trees. Palm trees, through no fault of their own, were some of Tessa's least favorite trees. (She had not known, for the majority of her life, that most people didn't have favorite and least favorite trees.) They were ubiquitous in the west and in the south, and were valued more as symbols for these places—Florida, Hollywood, Los Angeles—than as trees in and of themselves. They had been co-opted by postcards and murals, made trite by decades of commercialism and success.

As long as she could remember, Tessa had been fascinated by trees. Their size, their root systems, their often immense and unbelievable age. Sometimes it felt crippling that she was a person, a being made to experience the world in just a few predetermined ways. Her sensory organs—her eyes, mostly—closed certain things off to her. They reduced everything to what she could see, a life where all she could observe was all that there was. Maybe trees, with their dearth of sensory organs and visual stimuli, had a way of experiencing the world that was far deeper and more intelligent than humans'.

"Hey, we're talented," said Alistair. He had a way of guiding their conversations back to a more productive, positive note; it was one of the things Tessa had first admired about him. His ambition, his refusal (except, admittedly, on *his* breakdown nights) to give into despair. It made him seem older than the others, even though he, like Tessa, was only nineteen. "Don't you think so?"

Nico ignored him. "How can I even say I'm an adult?

I'm twenty-two, living in either a motel or an RV, depending on the week. I don't have a college education." At these words, Tessa's stomach gave a little twist, like a worm turning over. "I'm clinging onto the last tattered shreds of my hopes."

"Hey, that's a good line," said Emrys, the drummer. He was Welsh, with a thin build, vibrant red shoulder-length hair, and cloudy blue eyes. He was also trying to grow a beard, but his genes didn't seem to support this idea. "Tattered Shreds of Hopes. I'll write that down." He tapped it into his phone.

"It sounds a little long and melodramatic," said Tessa, coming back from the window. She sat down next to Alistair again, trying not to look at him. "No offense, Nico. Maybe we can cut it down to Tattered Hopes?"

Emrys sighed exaggeratedly. "Okay, okay, I'll put a note. *Tessa thinks it's too melodramatic.* I'll be sure to bring that up to Greg."

Greg, their booking agent, had not been in contact with them for months, but they all tended to ignore that. They spoke about him like he was a father who'd run out to the corner store to buy cigarettes and would be back shortly, despite having been at the corner store for three months now.

Nico's head lolled back against the couch, which was stained with what looked like grape juice or port wine. "Ugh. How is it only one a.m.? I feel like it's been one a.m. for hours now. It's like the morning will never come."

"Hey, that's even better! What about...The Morning Never Comes? Or The Morning Never Came?" Emrys began typing in great excitement.

"Fantastic title, but it's been done," said Tessa. "Swallow the Sun did it like ten years ago."

"Of course they did."

"What? It's not like anyone would notice," said Nico in despair. "Because no one'll freakin' hear our music anyway. What was the last show, like ten people?"

"That wasn't a show," said Alistair. "It was the tail end of someone's thirtieth birthday party where everyone was dopey and blasted enough to give us a chance."

"You're helping."

"I'm just being realistic."

"I'm sure that's what all the successful people said. *I'm just being realistic.* Yeah. That realistic, sober kind of attitude will get you far."

"I thought success isn't on the menu for us, Nico, or have you been talking about something else this whole time?"

"You're not supposed to freakin' agree with me! You're supposed to tell me I'm wrong and raise me up and—and support me!"

"I thought it was your parents' job to raise you up and support you," put in Zac, and at this Nico lunged across the carpet, picked up his empty beer can from where he'd thrown it, and threw it at him again. It bounced off his other knee.

"I'm tired." Alistair stretched his arms over his head, and his shirt rode up, exposing two inches of pale stomach. Tessa's eyes stuck there for a moment before she could drag them away.

"Me too," she said. This, the mention of being tired, was their private code, and her body buzzed as she spoke, a connection threading invisible underneath the noises of the others laughing and arguing and debating. The two of them finally managed to get the others out of the room: Nico slouching, his long neck bent like the stalk of a plucked flower, Zac smirking, and Emrys still tapping potential song titles into his phone.

Alistair called out good night and shut the door behind them. There was a moment before he turned around in which Tessa, sitting completely still, could feel the blood rushing through every part of her body. Coursing through the maze of her arteries, making U-turns at the ends of her fingers and toes, collecting and re-collecting in the chambers of her heart. This was how she imagined it, anyway. Around them: the hush of a motel at night. Underneath the stench of pot smoke, that blankness made up of the combined remnants of dozens of different people and belongings and lives and exhalations. You could find it in gas station stores, and Penn Station, and airport bathrooms. All those lives combining to make a not-smell, a sense of lack, the way all colors combined made brown, but not the brown of Alistair's eyes—this was a muddy, ugly brown. A brown somehow emptier and further from any color than even white or black was.

Alistair walked towards her, slipping in and out of shadow. She thought of jungles, light pouring through the canopy of leaves, although they were probably as far from a jungle as they could get. He sank down on the bed next to her; it gave beneath his weight. She thought, momentarily, of a stone sinking into water.

"So," he said.

"So," she said. Her voice was breathless and anticipatory, not at all like his, which was always the slightest bit cool, removed, sarcastic.

He waited for her to lean towards him, just the tiniest bit, before closing the gap and pushing her down onto the low, stained mattress.

Alistair and Tessa were the band's two singers. Most doom metal bands didn't have a female singer, but Pestilential Harbor did, and it was one of the things that separated them from all the other bands. Especially with a name like that, no one expected a woman to be part of their group. But Alistair covered the growls and snarls and Tessa took care of the soaring, operatic female vocals. She thought they worked well together. In fact, she'd always considered their voices to have a particularly intense chemistry. It wasn't just her, either; last year, a music writer had found them after one of their early shows and told them, her round face shining with enthusiasm, "Your voices blend together like those of an angel and a devil." Her voice shook with sincerity, and at that moment, Tessa had a vision of the two of them: Alistair mired in red light, looking up at Tessa, who was floating high above him, wreathed in a white glow. And at that moment, she could have sworn Alistair, who glanced at her for a second, had seen the same thing.

After that, her feelings about him changed. Sometimes when she watched performances of the band—they all did; Nico claimed he didn't, but he was definitely lying—and Alistair came onscreen, filling the video, she would be unable to stop her eyes from sliding away from him. She might have thought it was because she wasn't that interested in him after all, but it wasn't that. It was the opposite—he was too bright, too fascinating, to look at for more than a moment or two. Something in her mind crumpled before the overwhelm of his face: a blazing star, a blinding sky.

She tried to imagine someone feeling that way about her, but her first thought was: *Mental ward.*

Things went on as usual, and she tried to tell herself

that what they had was just vocal chemistry. Their voices meshed well together. Nothing else. But then, two months ago, Alistair found her after one of the shows. They were in the back of the bar, where the bands were supposed to wait before performing, but no one else was there—Zac and Emrys and Nico had gone outside for a smoke, and Alistair, who did not smoke, as it made him paranoid, had remained behind. Tessa had decided not to smoke that night either. She never felt like it after a performance; her throat was already sore from singing. It was all right for the others, who never sang or even opened their mouths during a performance, but the thought of inhaling pot smoke afterwards, of it sliding down her throat like gravel on flesh, made her queasy.

After that show Alistair's skin was glowing, pearlescent. They'd gotten the biggest turnout they'd had in months, and even though it was nothing compared to their early shows, it had, at the time, seemed like the beginning of something new. An upswing. He was sitting on a crate of sound equipment, silver daggers dangling from his ears. His face didn't bristle with piercings the way Nico's did—Nico was always tugging on his nose ring and running his tongue over his lip ring, which Tessa found nauseating—but he didn't shy away from jewelry the way Zac did. Tessa remembered Zac squealing, "No way, man! Necklaces are for girls!" when Alistair had offered to give him one of the metal chains he'd gotten. Alistair had simply shrugged and looped it over his own neck, where it jangled with the rest of his necklaces. Tessa found it wildly attractive, the way he celebrated his body and considered it worthy of adornment, adding decorations to it without the slightest bit of insecurity over how "girly" it might seem. Sometimes she could picture him as an ancient Egyptian pharaoh, looking out over his kingdom of pyramids and slaves, his body ornamented with heavy collars and bracelets and amulets, gold glimmering beneath a blistering sun.

Alistair looked at her, his body long and angular on top of the crate, a collection of geometric shapes. He said, "You were amazing," and she said, her heart still pounding from the performance, "No, *you* were amazing," and he said, "Why do you always argue so much?" and she came over closer to him so she could speak without needing to project too much and replied, "What are you talking about, I never argue, how absurd," and he just shook his head and stood up —becoming suddenly, dizzyingly taller than her—and kissed her.

They kissed until they remembered that there was a storage closet nearby, and they went inside. Tessa would never, ever tell him this, Alistair who had been with perhaps five or six women by the age of nineteen, but up until that moment, she was a virgin. He didn't seem to notice anything. When he had turned away to dispose of the condom, she wiped the blood away with her hand and, lacking anything to smear it on besides her own clothes, stuck it in her mouth. It tasted like any other blood, like the blood she'd sucked from very rare steak: metallic, warm. When he turned back to her she was no longer a virgin and she tasted the loss of this in her own mouth, smiling at him through it, through the dank and coppery tang.

Since then they had been hooking up in secret from time to time. In the RV it was impossible, of course, but the occasional stays in motels were welcome—although they stayed in motels less and less often these days as their performances dwindled. When they did, they always roomed together, because while Tessa was the band's only girl, she had to share her room with *someone,* and it made sense that the band's two singers share the same space—or at least, that was what she and Alistair told the others. ("It makes complete sense, from a perspective of artistic... *osmosis*," Emrys had agreed, nodding seriously.)

But they had to keep it under wraps. If the other members ever found out about the two of them, they'd lose their minds. Members of the same band getting romantically involved was a well-known curse. She could picture Nico saying, "Are you freakin' *kidding*?", his long face sagging with disappointment, and Emrys telling them in a quick, almost excited voice that *this* was why they hadn't booked any shows recently.

Now, she wondered if maybe Alistair had pushed Nico to book this motel because of her, because he wanted more time with her. There were other explanations, of course, reasons all of them wanted to stay in a motel: more room, more privacy, a change of scenery. But she couldn't stop herself from thinking this. Even after they went to sleep in separate beds—Alistair couldn't sleep next to anyone—and the room filled with his deep, slow breathing, he was present in two ways. There was his actual self, the one sleeping in the bed across the room, and there was the Alistair floating at the edges of Tessa's thoughts. There, he resembled the same Alistair she had imagined that night after the show when the music writer had complimented them: looking up at her from the glow of an alien red light, an expression of reverence on his angular face.

CHAPTER TWO

THE BRONX, NEW YORK, 2020

Carl and Tessa picked their way through the streets on their way to visit his mother. Along the way they passed multitudes of trash cans lying on their sides, tatters of fabric flapping in the breeze. It was not a refreshing breeze but a kind of exhalation, a moist breath spreading over the borough. Garbage dotted the sidewalk at intervals, rotting cardboard boxes and discarded blue medical masks, coffee cups flattened and falling apart. The heavy sog of early autumn clinging to their clothes. Rust and rain breaking everything down.

"I've asked her many times to move out," Carl was saying. "Get a nice place on Park Avenue, maybe, or Lexington Avenue if she thinks that's too ostentatious. She won't do it."

Tessa hadn't asked. Her father gave her this explanation every two years or so, whenever he brought her along to visit his ninety-one-year-old mother, Grise. Someone so old living all by herself was sad, but at least she wasn't entirely without company. Carl often visited her on his own, and Tessa's mother spoke to her on the phone every few weeks, despite the fact that they weren't related by blood. Even after the divorce, Holly had maintained this connection, calling the older woman up from California to talk about history and psychology and current events. As a cynical teenager, Tessa had suspected that this was a performative psychological trick of her mother's to make herself seem like a better person, perhaps even to get herself into Carl's good graces somehow, but she'd eventually realized: Holly genuinely enjoyed talking to her mother-in-law. It had nothing to do with Carl.

Tessa was long past the age where Carl could just cart her along to visit her grandmother. Today she had come out of willingness, as well as the fact that there was not much else to do when she visited her father. Since she had graduated college, she'd begun living in San Diego, and had taken the time she spent with each of her parents into her own hands. She had the freedom to do so, since she worked remotely, so her weeks with her father in New York were spent like this: during the day he would go to work on Wall Street and she would open her laptop and begin her own work in the empty, sunwashed apartment. Her father would come home in the evening and they would either order food or eat the leftovers from the previous day. When they ate he was gregarious and enthusiastic, asking questions about her job that implied it was much more interesting than it really was. She could also always count on him to impart some obscure piece of knowledge about the food, like "One ravioli is called a *raviolo*, did you know that?" or "We couldn't have any Italian prosciutto imported here throughout all of the seventies and eighties, all the way up till '89, because it was banned. That's why we were all so decadent—we were trying to replace the gaping hole left in our lives by the lack of prosciutto." She was fairly certain that he made some of these facts up.

"Why won't she move out?" Tessa asked now, although she had heard the answer many times before.

"She says she's not comfortable living somewhere new. Especially since the pandemic began. She says she's too old by now to make a start somewhere else, let alone handle all the stress of moving."

"But she'll have to eventually, right?"

Carl looked at her like he didn't understand.

"I mean...when she gets really old..." Tessa searched for the words to say this in a non-offensive way. "Won't she have to live somewhere like a home, an assisted living center?"

Carl's face clouded with disgust. "I can afford a live-in nurse for her if she gets to that stage," he said. "I don't want her ending up at one of those awful places. Where everything smells like cabbage and sulfur and everyone is just waiting for you to die."

Tessa was momentarily shocked into silence. "I just meant somewhere she could feel safe," she managed. "Like, get help if she fell or something."

"She's never wanted to leave. Ever since my dad died, I tried to get her out of that place. But something about it comforts her. Because it was the place where I grew up, I guess, the place where she had a home and a family for the majority of her life." His voice had grown thinner, stretched out, and he stopped talking as they waited to cross the street. A fire truck blared by, sirens wailing, and they watched it pass, the sound fading downwards in frequency as it disappeared into the distance. "The time for them to move was before he died, but they couldn't afford it, and I wasn't making enough back then to be able to help them."

They passed a single-block park, and Tessa noted the scraggly overgrown weeds, the crumpled fast food bags and soda cans. A few empty benches stood further inside, graffiti standing out on the wood like a clumsy attempt at camouflage.

"I used to be terrified of that place when I was a kid," Carl said, nodding towards the park. "There were all these mangy stray cats. Rats, too. Huge ones. And later, people passed out all over the ground and the benches with needles in their arms. It was one of those places you avoided."

"Nobody's there anymore," she pointed out. "I don't see any cats, though, either." She was always conscious of how much younger she became when speaking to her father, moving backwards in time, peppering him with questions like an eight-year-old. Her father never seemed to notice; these days he spoke to her as though she was an adult like him. Maybe it was because she was older now, not a kid or a teenager or even a young adult really but a fully-fledged Adult, which probably made her father think they were on more equal footing and could talk about things with a new peer-to-peer closeness they had not experienced before. But Tessa did not share this belief. She did not feel like an Adult at all, and looking back now, it was strange how she had felt more like an adult as a seventeen-year-old than she did now at twenty-five.

She remembered what she had been like on the road with Pestilential Harbor (what an idiotic name; even thinking of it made her cringe), barely legal but playing shows that filled rooms. How powerful she had felt then, as though it was her presence that had caused their fullness. *Bullshit*, she thought. It had not been her presence, or even Alistair's, or anyone else's. It had been down to time and luck and circumstance, which had ultimately come together in Alistair's favor. At least for a while.

"I haven't seen anything alive there for years," her father was saying, still looking towards the park. "Maybe the occasional rat."

"Where did all those people go?"

"Dead or in jail."

"What about the cats?"

He chuckled. "Probably dead or in jail too."

As they walked, Tessa noticed the trees on the sidewalk, as she always did when visiting New York. They seemed to be planted fewer and further between than they had been last time, or the time before that—but of course that was impossible. The holes in the concrete hadn't changed. Maybe it was only the shapes of the trees themselves that forced this illusion: they were stunted, even twisted, as though the ground were gradually pulling some vital life force out of them. An unsettling image came to her of a future where the trees would be only a few feet tall, shrunken into black, lifeless husks, like small burned skeletons. With some effort, she forced the thought out of her mind.

They crossed the street to Grise's apartment. The lobby was dimly lit, and on the other side was what looked like a metal cage over the mailboxes. A long, stained mirror showed Tessa her bloated face, full of water weight gained from the pills she was taking; she looked away.

Upstairs, Grise called from the other room that she would be there in a minute. In the sitting room, which was really the kitchen and dining room and living room combined into one, Tessa noticed a layer of dust on everything. It was present even on the dining room table, with a few marks in it, small interruptions caused by the movement of plates and dishes. When she put her finger to it, the tip came away fuzzy and gray, as though covered in a coat of mold. She wiped her hand surreptitiously on her jeans.

It looked like nobody had cleaned anything in weeks. There was hair in the carpet, and from what she could see of the sink something had splashed in it—milk? cream?—and been allowed to dry. There was a smell, too, what Tessa was learning was the distinctive old-person smell: the scent of the proteins in the body breaking down.

Grise came out of the other room. She moved slowly and carefully, with the built-in caution of someone who has long since forgotten the time when her limbs could crash against a doorframe and be counted on to withstand the impact. As long as Tessa had known her, her grandmother had been an old woman. Even when she'd held Tessa as a baby, twenty-five years ago, Grise Tanner had never been anything else. The only difference was that since then she had gotten older, and frailer, and slower.

"Mom," Carl said. "You've got to let me set you up with a cleaning lady."

"No, no. I can take care of everything myself. I'm only cleaning up after one person." She smiled, revealing teeth that were translucent and thunderstorm-gray. She had white hair curled in the old 1950s style, and wore a loose pair of pants and a pastel purple sweater. Liver spots covered her hands, creeping up into her wrists and into her sleeves like invading insects. The lines on her face, spider-webbed through the jowls that looked like some of the only fat left on her body, had grown deeper, and underneath her outfit her figure looked shapeless, skeletal: just bones and the gaps between them, bones and negative space.

Tessa glanced over at her father, wondering why he didn't appear more alarmed. She was pretty sure her grandmother hadn't looked this bad the last time they'd been here. But it was true that on that occasion, Tessa hadn't paid attention to much outside of her own head. She'd still been preoccupied with her own fate, halfway through her first semester of college at the time and despondent at the fact that it was everything she had feared: judgmental cliques; obnoxious, screaming sorority girls; rapist frat boys; mistakes you made once and could never take back and which marked you for eternity.

"Yes, but it can be very hard work to take care of an entire apartment," Carl said. "I saw Holly struggling to do it when we had our place in New York, and you're over ninety. A cleaning lady would be a great help for you. Whaddaya say, Mom?"

"Cleaning lady," Grise repeated in disdain. "Women never needed help with these things back when I was young. They did everything themselves."

Carl inhaled, and Tessa could guess what he was thinking: Back then, people didn't live as long. Or if they did, they lived with their families to help take care of them.

But Grise maintained her knowing, superior gaze, not revealing a flicker of embarrassment. Maybe she couldn't see the dust properly, maybe her eyes were physically not good enough to discern the layers of filth that had collected on the spout of the faucet, the top of the refrigerator.

Grise asked Tessa how she was finding life after college. Tessa quailed at admitting how much she'd hated college, how much she still hated the thought of it, how the jobs she'd gotten as a result of it had been mind-numbing and soul-destroying, grinding her spirit down like a piece of wood on a rock. Instead she pretended that it was great, that she was finding all the opportunities before her incredibly challenging and really rewarding. In fact, she said "really rewarding" twice in the same sentence. Somehow she managed to spin the drudgery of her remote data entry job into a "multifaceted opportunity for engagement." Then she accidentally mixed in language she'd seen in job postings, saying that the job enabled her to "wear many hats." (At this, Grise looked like she didn't know what the hell Tessa was talking about.) She was acutely aware of Carl watching her out of the corner of his eye with that wobbly-mouthed expression that meant he was barely holding back a smirk.

When Tessa finished, trailing off at the end of one of her more nonsensical sentences, Grise smiled. This time her mouth was closed, and her near lack of lips, the almost-straight line of them, made Tessa think momentarily of a knitting wound.

Grise leaned forwards and said, still smiling, "We all know that is a load of *Müll*, right?"

"What?"

"Garbage."

"Well," Tessa said. She fought back the urge to laugh. "Well, maybe you're right."

Grise smiled wider and wider, looked sideways at her son. He was grinning, too, and finally started laughing. "You can't fool Mom!" he said. "Good try, Tessa, but she's a lot sharper than those guidance counselors they lined you up in front of at USC."

"My husband Allen, your grandfather, didn't like college much either. He saw education as a means to an end, rather than something to enjoy in and of itself. He didn't enjoy his job overmuch either, although he of course enjoyed providing for his family. Your father has told me about your job, and while I'm sure he's proud of you for it, *he* never gave any indication that you found it excessively rewarding or fulfilling in any way." Grise shook her head. "I'm truly not certain why you young people are acting like your jobs are the only thing you ever wanted. Is this how it is now, the way things work these days? It's okay to want other things, you know."

"I guess it's kind of the way things work right now," Tessa said. "You've got to pretend that the activity of inputting numbers into spreadsheets is all you ever dreamed of in your entire life, that nothing would make you happier than slaving away underneath some immense, monolithic corporation until you..." She caught herself just in time, face burning: she had been about to say *Until you're too old to do anything useful, and then you die.* Jesus. What was wrong with her? Had college and work and her narrow *Career Path* burned away all her self-awareness, all of her empathy?

"Tessa," Carl said in surprise. "Why don't you ever tell me these things?" He was joking, of course. She had said many things of this nature.

"A spreadsheet," Grise repeated. "I'm not familiar with what that is, but it doesn't sound pleasant."

"It's not."

They were silent for a minute,

"You know my mother's favorite motto?"

"No..."

"I'll teach you some German."

"That was her motto?"

She laughed. "No. Although—can you imagine? No, her motto was, *Mach dir keine Sorgen über Dinge, die du nicht ändern kannst.*" The words sounded like mounds of sand leaving her mouth, in her gray, aging voice, vocal cords slack with age. "Or: *Don't worry about things you can't change.*"

Tessa had already forgotten pretty much everything but the first word, like the German was an Etch-A-Sketch that had been shaken. She tried to recall the rest of it anyway—*die? dir?*—but then she noticed that her grandmother's face had frozen in a startled frown.

"Mom?" Carl leaned forward.

"That was my father's motto," she said slowly. She looked confused now, as though wondering how she could possibly have made such a mistake. "I must have forgotten."

"It's okay," Carl said. But Tessa saw a shadow of his mother's expression on his face, confusion and alarm.

Carl and Tessa ended up cleaning the entire sitting room and kitchen. Grise puttered around, trying to help, but when she dropped a tray of silverware, Carl forced her to sit down. "Take it easy," he said. "We're here to help you, not make your life harder."

"Oh, is that why you came?" she asked, her tone dry, half-sardonic. "To help, not because you wanted to see me?"

"Of course not, Mom. But that's part of it. Please, sit down. Pretend it's Mother's Day."

"Every day is Mother's Day in spirit," she said, but she did as she was told, sitting carefully down on the couch, which was itself dusty. Tessa almost thought she saw a little white cloud poof up as her grandmother sat.

They ate dinner, which Carl ordered; when his mother protested, he insisted, sweeping out his credit card with the smooth movement of someone who did this all the time.

"Chinese okay?" Carl asked Tessa.

She hesitated, then remembered it didn't matter anyway. She wasn't going to text Josh, and her chances of running across a hot guy in New York in the next few days, holed up with her father, were extremely slim. "Just something low-sodium for me," she said. "Chicken with broccoli, I guess, light on the sauce." When she noticed Grise looking at her, she explained, not even sure why she was telling her this: "I'm trying to limit my salt. My face has gotten kind of chubby lately." The antidepressants had the annoying side effect of plumping her face up, making everything bigger: her eyelids, her cheeks, even her nose. They took every drop of water she drank and shuttled it to a place directly beneath her skin.

Grise shook her head, but not like she had before, with impatience. Now she shook it slowly and sadly. "You are so beautiful," Grise said. Her tone was mournful, expansive, huge swathes of ink. "You are so beautiful." She had the voice and expression of someone pressing their hands against a glass they could not break through.

Tessa was less than one-third of her grandmother's age, and compared to her she was at the beginning of her youth. Grise's proclamation of how beautiful she was had not seemed insincere. Tessa had already learned that people noticed what you had in comparison to what they did not have. Her own mother, for example: Holly had often proclaimed how thick Tessa's hair was, and only when Tessa was a little older did she realize how thin her mother's hair had become, and this was why she *oohe*d and *aahe*d over Tessa's hair despite Tessa (and everyone else) never really noticing. And her constantly-working father often remarked on how lucky she was to have so much free time.

When it came to the idea of beauty, she was used to friends and relatives throwing out the words *beautiful* or *gorgeous* or *pretty* regardless of whether they were true (one of her college friends' mothers had unthinkingly called her "gorgeous" when she was in the midst of a disfiguring allergic reaction, and clapped her hand to her mouth immediately afterwards).

But this was different. For Grise, beautiful did not mean the same thing it meant to Tessa, or even to her college friend's mother. For Tessa and other people her age, *beautiful* was a synonym for several different qualities in one combination or another: slenderness, athleticism, youth, happiness, mental and physical health. But for her grandmother, the other qualities had fallen away years ago: youth was the only one left that mattered. Tessa was not especially healthy or happy, but these things were afterthoughts for Grise. Tessa was still young, far from the end of her own journey across the earth, and to her grandmother, this was all it took for her to be beautiful.

The pills Tessa was taking had been prescribed to her the previous spring, when she'd graduated college. She had gotten them from a hard-faced, soft-voiced psychiatrist, upon learning of Tessa's feelings of emptiness. She had described it to him as "feeling a blankness, but if I focus I can sense the sadness rushing below it, like a river under a frozen layer of ice." As soon as she said it she thought the metaphor overdramatic, laughable even, but he just nodded and folded his hands together. She never saw him take any notes. He was like the psychiatrist version of one of those waiters who never wrote down your order but simply kept it all in their head.

She'd started seeing him midway through her senior year but had refused to take any pills until it became clear that her depression wasn't going away when she graduated. "I don't want to take pills *because* of college," she said, when she first started seeing him. She hadn't wanted to, but her father had urged her to, insisting that he could afford it, and even Holly was growing concerned about her daughter's listlessness and lack of affect. ("Oh, even *Holly*," Tessa had imitated at this point, irritated by how her father never referred to her mother as "your mother," but only spoke of her by her first name, as though refusing to raise her to the position of *mother* in Tessa's eyes. "I guess that's how we know it's *really* serious.")

"Why do you think college is making you depressed?" the psychiatrist asked.

"I'm scared it's not. I'm scared that this isn't going to go away in three months when I graduate."

She'd been right. It hadn't.

Now, it was the beginning of the 2020s. She still wasn't sure why exactly she was on the pills. What the problem was in her brain that made her need to take them. Her life was fine, on paper. Luckily for her, she had weathered the COVID-19 pandemic and the resulting aftershocks fairly well. She had a data-entry job where she could work from home, and it didn't pay oodles and oodles of money but it paid enough. She lived in an apartment in San Diego that she shared with two roommates, and it had lots of light, big windows, a scattering of succulents on the sills. She wasn't entirely sure why she was depressed. Nothing was really going wrong in her life. She had friends, a job, a good relationship with both of her parents.

Ironically, the time in her life when she'd been most sure of her happiness was also the most unmoored time in her life. The time during which she'd been least connected to anyone or anything, where her future might be good or bad: an expansive, brilliantly lit stage, or a bottomless lake waiting to swallow her.

Tessa flew home a few days later. And although this happened every time, it never ceased to surprise her: as soon as she stepped out of the swooshing glass doors of the air-conditioned San Diego Airport, the midday heat enveloped her like another layer of clothing. The sensation wasn't claustrophobic, although she knew it probably should feel that way. Rather, it was comforting. *Home*, she thought.

Holly was waiting outside the airport, leaning against the wall and smoking. She waved when she saw Tessa, tossed her cigarette to the ground, and together they walked to Holly's car.

"How are things with your dad?" Holly asked as they began driving.

"They're fine. We got lots of Italian food. How are things here?"

"Shit, Tessa. I forgot to tell you." Her hands tightened on the wheel, the skin on her knuckles stretched tight over white knobs of bone. "There's a wildfire in the Six Rivers National Forest. It's been going on for four days. About a million acres are gone so far."

"A *million?*"

"That's less than a quarter of what burned a couple years ago. But the fire's just started, so. Who knows how it will end up. They think it may have been caused by a lightning strike," Holly added, clearly prepared for the question Tessa had just been about to ask. "Or maybe even arson. It definitely wasn't a prescribed burn that got out of control. That much, they're insisting on."

Tessa looked out her window, as though she might see flames right next to the highway. She felt nauseous again at the idea of all that forestry destroyed: leaves upon leaves, decades of growth, the homes of countless animals. The one comforting thought was that it might have been lightning that had caused it, not direct human activity—but then again, all these fires *were* caused by human activity, by climate change. Even lightning strikes only burned the amount of forest they did because everything was so hot and arid now, because the fire season had grown so unnaturally long.

And the thought of arson, of someone deliberately dropping the match that would torch countless acres of trees, was even more sickening. In the years that had elapsed since Pestilential Harbor had disintegrated—in the years since Tessa had taken all the steps she'd once sworn she never would—the natural world was one of the few things that had seemed to hold steady. Like her parents and her grandmother, it had been the backdrop of her life, a scenery that never changed.

But her grandmother was starting to lose her memory, or rather her mind, and the forests were being eaten up by fire, by heat, by relentless flame. And even Tessa, even her parents—all of them were aging. All of them, in turn, were being burnt away by time.

She swallowed and pressed her forehead to the glass, hoping it would cool her skin and calm her, but all it did was jostle her brain inside her skull. "How did I not hear about this?"

"Probably because you've been in New York. They don't care about that kind of stuff over there. All they're interested in is money money money, how much they can make and how many people they can screw over while pretending they're not."

"I don't think that's necessarily true," Tessa said, but her mother was already on a roll.

"Your dad's got something of a savior complex, you know. All those hours he spends trading, it's made him think he's actually accomplishing something and helping the world. Sunk cost fallacy. If he didn't maintain the illusion that he was keeping the earth spinning, he'd collapse."

"Mom. Can you stop? You've been doing this since I was a kid."

"Oh, and he hasn't?" Her mother's voice was strident, challenging.

Tessa recalled how her father never used the words *your mother*, how he left Holly out of every possible conversation he could. But then, he never directly shit-talked Holly to her either.

"Just please stop," she said.

Holly sighed through her nose. "Okay. Sure. How was your flight?"

"There was some turbulence at the beginning. A lot, actually. At first I thought I might be one of those people who has a bad experience on a plane gets scared of flying... and then the turbulence got worse, and I started thinking that I might not actually *live* to be one of those people..." She laughed, but her mother must have heard how forced it was, how Tessa's throat was still tight with the echo of fear, because when Holly looked over at her next, her forehead was creased in worry. There was an utterly unself-conscious tenderness in her eyes, too, so similar to what Tessa saw in her father's that she had to look away. She felt the old frustration rising up in her, so deep-set that it was like a reflex by now, that familiar question: Her parents both loved her, so why couldn't they just stay *together* and love her? (This was a question from an age when she'd been so self-centered that it had seemed to her that the only possible reason for a parent existing was to love their child.)

Her parents both loved her, that was true. They just didn't love each other. Tessa had learned this when she was five years old, when her parents told her they were divorcing. They hadn't used that word back then, had stuck to words like *separating* and, when this still produced confusion, *leaving. Moving apart.* Even now she remembered the atmosphere, how brittle and tense it was, the way her parents always stopped talking whenever she came into the room.

She had gone through a phase of wishing she was an octopus, so she could use her long, strong arms to hold her parents tight next to her and not let them go. This was right around the time her octopus fascination had begun, prompted by a picture book her mother gave her for her fifth birthday. The book was about Willie the octopus and all his friends, whom he reeled in whenever he was feeling lonely (thinking about it now, it was slightly creepy the way no one could escape Willie and his grasping tentacles). At this point, she'd thought that her parents, forced into physical closeness by her cephalopod hug, would have no choice but to realize they still loved each other after all. They would relax into Tessa's tentacles, and they would be a family again. This was when Tessa was young and stupid, her interpretation of the world shaped by nothing more than her own experiences, back when she thought proximity was the only thing necessary for love.

CHAPTER THREE

BARSTOW, CALIFORNIA, 2014

One thing Tessa was certain of: if she had gone to college, she would have hated it. She'd known this since her junior year of high school, when Mrs. Copeland, the college advisor, had stepped out of the shadows from where she had been lurking in the eleventh-floor office, and smiled, revealing teeth that were a darker shade than her skin. Nobody had really known Mrs. Copeland before this time, seeing her only as a distant, curly-haired figure at the end of a hallway or at the staff table in the cafeteria, but now that they were in junior year, it was time to get acquainted with her. She began giving them college talks and inviting them to Consider Their Futures and imagining what their Career Paths would be. Tessa, seventeen and already dripping with suspicion, listened to these talks with crossed arms and a sneer twitching the corner of her lip. *Career Path*, she thought, as Mrs. Copeland smiled her smile of cracked, margarine-colored teeth. What a stupid name for a future. It hinted at a narrow and straightforward road where you had to keep your elbows tucked and your gaze fixed firmly ahead—not the boundless field of possibilities adults had always told you you'd run through, shouting in joy with arms akimbo. Yes, maybe they initially promised you that your future would be limitless, but the name they actually gave it told you what it would *really* be.

Another thing Tessa had observed: it didn't seem to matter which career path you chose. Once you went to college, all the paths tended to be the same. They all locked you into a seat behind a desk, ass growing molded to the contours of your chair, eyes growing small and bloodshot, heart growing tight and cold and mean. She had witnessed this in everyone she knew over the age of thirty—or, when she really thought about it, over the age of twenty-five.

At the start of her senior year, Tessa let her parents know she wasn't going to college. It was chaos. At first her mother spoke to her in a calm and serious tone, like they were friends having an important (but friendly!) discussion. When this proved ineffectual, she switched tactics, lecturing Tessa about the emptiness of her future, and finally moved to wheedling. When none of these methods succeeded in making a dent in Tessa's decision, she eventually shouted at her daughter until the color drained from her face and her freckles stood out like scars. "Not a very good tactic for a psychologist," Tessa pointed out, and at this, Holly stormed from the room and locked herself in her bedroom for the night.

Shortly after this, Tessa was shuttled off across the country to New York, where her father got weekend custody of her. Carl picked up where her mother had left off. He was less variable than Holly in his tone: throughout the entire weekend, he informed Tessa in a stern and hectoring tone about her prospects (few), her decision (rash), and her prefrontal cortex development (incomplete). By the end of the weekend, Tessa's mind had only been made up more firmly to not go to college and not become the pathetic and manipulative wrecks her parents had. She flew back from New York to California and right into the eye of her mother's anger, which had only grown more intense during the time Tessa was on the East Coast.

That week-long fight became, in Tessa's mind, the stuff of legend. She even got an idea for a new song—Splattered Chaos—but Emrys had vetoed it, saying that any song stemming from an argument with one's parents would bring with it the odor of teen malcontent and be too juvenile for their audience.

By that point she had been in the band for seven months. She had been taking vocal lessons and training with a coach for nearly the same amount of time, spending the money she made at her shitty job at PacSun, working harder than she'd ever worked on anything in her life. They hadn't gotten their agent yet—they only signed with Greg in the first days of 2013, at which point they actually began booking venues for shows. But they were playing and recording nearly every day, dizzy with the excitement of creating something, and Tessa's future looked like it was expanding out before her in a glorious golden haze.

They had begun in February of 2012, in Nico's garage —literally in a garage—because Nico had the biggest place and the most space for them. They got the idea for it at Tessa's birthday party, and though she didn't like to admit it even to herself, this was one of the reasons she had always thought of the band as more *hers* than anyone else's (even though it was Alistair's face on the center of their posters, Alistair's name before hers on every announcement): because it had begun as a celebration for her, of her.

At her birthday party, it had been her and Emrys and

Madison and Emma and Nico—all of whom were also in their junior years, except Nico, who hadn't done much with himself since graduating two years ago, but he did provide a generous space in which to hold the party. He was the older friend they all liked to introduce to their parents to see the looks on their faces. Holly was more tolerant of these things than some of the other mothers, who looked like they'd swallowed a live goldfish upon seeing Nico's piercings and long shaggy hair.

After the cake had been eaten and the candles blown out and the congratulations given—"You're seventeen!" Madison crowed. "You're now legal in six states!"—they'd begun poking around in the back of the garage, discovering the instruments there. Nico had revealed, shyly, that he liked to play bass in his spare time, and then Emrys said something about drumming and writing poetry, which was basically writing lyrics, wasn't it, and Emma had looked from one of them to the other and said, "This is incredible! You should start a band!"

And Tessa, hazy with beer and cake and the thrill of turning seventeen (and of becoming legal in six states), thought that this was the idea of the century.

All day the traffic outside the motel droned on like a murmur, a restless unbroken sound. The nights were cool, but the mornings and afternoons pulsed with heat, heat so intense it was almost visible. It *was* visible sometimes—the gleaming pools of water she saw at the furthest points of roads, mirages that winked at her and vanished when she walked closer.

It was noon, and the sun was at its zenith. With only

snacks in the motel room, dusty bags of chips and crackers and plastic-tasting bottles of water, they decided to walk to the nearby diner. The parking lot of this particular motel was one of the most desolate places Tessa had ever seen: doomed weeds struggling up through cracked pavement even as they turned brittle and yellow. Sweat poured down her face. She thought, *If I were in college I'd be in an air-conditioned classroom right now.*

But then Alistair smiled at her, a secret smile that she only ever saw him give her, and she thought, *Yeah, I'd be in an air-conditioned classroom taking notes on some obscure theory by a dead white man, without a thought in my head other than how to memorize it and regurgitate it back onto an exam.*

At least the diner was air-conditioned, too. They sat in a booth up against the window, through which she could see the shapes of the cars in the parking lot, brittle and shiny like emptied-out exoskeletons. Separate from the cool inside of the diner, they swam in a heat haze.

Nico didn't even look at the menu, instead asking for "an iced coffee, no sweetener or milk, please." He raised his sunglasses to ask, as though this would help the server understand him, and then put his sunglasses back down, lowered his hat, and slouched against the wall behind him.

"Why are you always eating salads?" Zac asked Emrys, once he had ordered.

"First of all, I like salads. Second of all, we need to maintain our ratios. It's something I've figured out, a visual component of Pestilential Harbor. Tessa is the girl, so that's obvious. And Alistair is her counterpart, the brooding male singer. But the rest of us, we represent more transcendental things—ideas rather than people. I'm the pale, skinny one, which means I represent the gentle side of death. I'm the essence of it in its most soft, natural, ethereal form. The kind of death that eases the suffering and the ancient from their pain."

"Kind of like The Easing of Torment?" Zac said, referring to one of their recent songs. Tessa couldn't tell whether he was being mocking or sincere. His eyebags, which never seemed to go away, looked almost purple in the diner's sallow light.

"Exactly. Nico, on the other hand," Emrys said, nodding at Nico, who was slumped motionless next to him, "he's a lot rougher-looking. Less natural—you know, with all his piercings and everything. He's a representation of the harsher, starker, more unnatural side of death, the kind of death that sweeps young and healthy people away in the blink of an eye."

"Jesus," Nico snapped. He raised a hand to his nose, as though to push his sunglasses up again, and then abruptly lowered it. "You're really going heavy on the metaphors like you think it'll make a difference. What, you think if you starve yourself then people will point you out and be like, *Ooh, look at that pale skinny guy, he's the embodiment of death, how deep, I'm sure glad we came to this show?*"

Emrys took a deep, measured breath and then pushed it out, not looking at Nico.

"I mean, go ahead and eat lettuce all day, we'll save money that way at least. But for god's sake, don't torture yourself in pursuit of an aesthetic that literally nobody is going to notice. We already look ridiculous playing doom metal in one of the hottest states in the country. If they look at you they won't think you're the embodiment of death, they'll think you're the embodiment of emaciation caused by heat stroke."

"If only we could go to Finland," Zac said, glancing

back and forth between the two of them. "Then we wouldn't have a problem with the climate at all. We'd blend right into the atmosphere. Yeah, we'd definitely be more successful somewhere like Finland."

Nico said, "Why are you looking at me?"

"I wasn't!" But he had been. They had all looked at Nico, in fact.

"Guys, look," Nico said. This time he did take his sunglasses off, placing them on the table and leaning forward on his elbows. His piercings dangled from his face; this gave them the illusion of having become immensely heavy, dragging him earthwards. "I know you think of me as, like, the Prince of Sheba. The Queen of the Nile. Whatever. But I don't actually have the money to keep us going forever. You've noticed that, right? You've seen how we've gone from three-star motels to, well, that?" He gestured at the parking lot outside the window. "Soon we won't be able to stay in motels at all. We aren't even on the road anymore, not technically. We're closer to being freakin' homeless than anything else."

"Don't say that," said Alistair. "That's a horrible attitude to have." There was something overly paternal about his tone, even though he was younger than Nico, and hearing it made Tessa's stomach sink. Her father's face floated into her mind like a reflex, shadowy and nearly featureless, like an insect silhouetted against a lightbulb. Three thousand miles from here and forever disappointed in her.

"I'm *just being realistic*," Nico said in a jagged, mocking tone. Clearly he hadn't forgotten their argument the other night. That was the thing about Nico: even with all the drugs, he never forgot anything. He was like a skinny, heavily pierced elephant, blowing weed smoke out of a shrunken trunk.

The server loomed over their table, plates of food in her hands. "Salad, burger, Caprese sandwich, chicken," she sang. She deposited their meals in front of them. Tessa's Caprese sandwich looked like it had been made ten years ago, and then frozen, microwaved, and sat on for good measure. The bread had the soft, spongey texture of the carpet in their motel room.

"Has anyone heard from Greg?" Tessa asked. They asked this often, twice a week or so, as though the topic of Greg were a ball they were passing around the circle, from one person to the next.

Everyone shook their heads.

Alistair leaned back. "I think it's time to think about booking a show ourselves."

"Ourselves?" Tessa asked. She was slightly annoyed at how he didn't look at her even when she said this, even though they were seated right next to each other; he just continued, speaking to the group, "Yeah. I've been doing some research, and there's this venue just in the next town that might be able to take us. It's called The Shot Glass. It used to be a punk space, but it's since expanded to host some other types of shows, and I think we might be able to fit in well with the theme."

"When were you going to tell us about this?" Nico demanded.

Alistair exhaled through his nose, looked down at the table. "I don't know why you guys always wait for me to tell you stuff. You're part of the band too. Every one of us is capable of doing our own research."

Even though he wasn't speaking directly to her, Tessa felt the beginnings of shame fill her. In the last few months, since the gigs had begun drying up, she'd been moving on autopilot, waiting for things to get better. Greg was one component, someone to wait for, but he had long since disappeared.

"Are you sure we're ready?" Emrys said. "We haven't finished ironing out the kinks in Maiden of Doom yet."

"And what about the fees?" Nico took a long sip of his coffee. "How big is this place?"

"When's the soonest we can book?" Tessa asked.

Alistair looked at her, finally, smiling a little. "Does next week work for everyone? Unless, of course, you have prior commitments." Hers was the only question he'd bothered to answer, and this time she felt like she was the one looking up at him through a shining, liquid light.

CHAPTER FOUR

SAN DIEGO, CALIFORNIA, 2021

Holly had been right, in a way. The fires did not continue to burn much longer, because it was already autumn. They died down shortly after Tessa got back to San Diego, and over the next few months, she relaxed into her life and stopped worrying about the larger world. She even stopped hearing the ticking of the doomsday clock inside her head, the ticking that sometimes felt nearly constant.

But the following summer the fires blazed into existence again, swallowing up five million acres of forest. It was all over the news: swathes of Big Basin and Santa Cruz destroyed, ancient old-growth forests torched to cinders. Places where Tessa had spent long, sprawling childhood summers, paddling through the lakes at sleepaway camp, gazing at the massive trees on the opposite shore—nothing left.

Upon learning of the fires, the first thing Tessa did was run to her laptop and type *is methuselah still alive*. The tree was on the opposite side of the state from the fires, but she still had to search for it, had to find out. When she saw no evidence of it being damaged in the fires, she relaxed in her chair in relief, just as she had the previous autumn.

The existence of this tree had long been a source of fascination to her. Like octopuses, it was a near-alien life form. But it was much older than any octopus, much older and still alive: it was nearly five thousand years old. When she'd learned of the year it had first germinated—2,833 B.C.—she had sat at her computer screen, barely breathing, her mind blank with shock. She could barely conceive of a living being that was five hundred years old, let alone five thousand.

Over two thousand years before Christ, she'd thought. *Further away from him than he was from us.* Tessa didn't believe in god, not really—no one she knew did, besides her grandmother—but the Biblical days formed a useful benchmark for civilization and the progression of time. She still preferred the terms *BC* and *AD* to *BCE* and *CE,* although she had barely been around at the time the former was still in widespread use.

Methuselah. It had existed long before the Romans; it had been written into Genesis in the form of a man. It had existed before the Bible, before even the Old Testament was recorded by the Hebrews on leather and animal skins. It loomed out of the shadows of the Stone Age, peering into the dawn of Egypt and the days of its first kings: kings from so long ago that their faces were visible not in paintings or sarcophagi but only chipped blocks of stone.

She looked up photos of it from time to time. The tree was short and stumpy and heavily gnarled, less a tree than a knotted mass of wood. Its body and limbs were thick, but at their zeniths they sprouted into tiny thornlike offshoots of their parents, spears of wood that resembled the last visible spirals of a fractal: a perfect recursion. The lines that stretched along its length were wavy, oceanic, as entrenched as the lines of minerals that wound through fossils. It wrung against itself, its limbs contorting one way and then the other as it wrapped around and around, more tightly twisted than a double helix. Methuselah was a shape emerging from the clouded depths of history, and she could see so much of nature in it—the curling spires of shells, the windswept dunes of the Sahara—that sometimes she had to look away from her screen, a knot forming in her throat at its sheer beauty.

Tessa had never seen it in person. She knew that its location was kept secret. She knew why this was: because there were many people, most of them men, who would love nothing more than to destroy the oldest single living thing on the planet. As though this would grant them, too, some form of immortality.

Tessa's roommates were named Pearl and Jupiter. Pearl was Korean, with laughing eyes and hair that shone like glossy dark water. Jupiter was British, and although he hadn't lived in England long enough to develop an accent—his parents had moved to America before he even developed the capacity for speech—he often used British slang and put on an accent, either Cockney or posh depending on his mood. He had tattoos and long white-dyed hair. He sometimes lit incense and sang along to operas in the middle of the night, which was fine with Pearl and Tessa, because they often stayed up all night too, and even joined in sometimes. He wore shirts until they developed holes and then wore them even more, even as he bemoaned the sexism that allowed men to wear holey shirts but not women (when Pearl brought up the fishnet top she often wore, a top which was mostly hole, he pretended not to hear). He once pierced his own ear with a safety pin and yelled into the sink, blood dripping down his hands: "I did it! I did it! Bloody *fuck*, that hurts!"

Jupiter and Pearl both worked from home as well. When she wasn't hiring and firing people over the internet —mostly firing—Pearl cooked, as if she believed her creations would ease the suffering she contributed to: enormous piles of fluffy pancakes, glazed salmon, roasted root vegetables. Jupiter, when not doing tech work online, performed in several experimental theater productions, often playing the role of someone who could only speak in grunts and murmurs, or a creature that bounded across the stage, barking riddles and dragging a many-colored tail.

At one point, he asked Tessa to watch him practice and give feedback—hesitantly, with plenty of reassurance that she didn't have to if she didn't have time. But she was happy to do it, because watching Jupiter rehearse was enchanting. Over the last few months of 2021, she watched him perform dozens of rehearsals right there in their living room. He would use household props to represent other actors: he'd ask a chair how it was doing, would lecture the microwave about communism. Some nights, he would practice a speech that was so heartbreaking that it made Tessa's throat close up. Other nights, he would throw out jokes so quickly that her stomach muscles cramped from ceaseless laughing.

Jupiter's face and voice were marvels, moldable and

evocative, representing the whole range of human emotions —and, it seemed, even some that stretched outside of that range. Sitting on the lumpy purple couch, Tessa would watch him perform his magic tricks. It was like watching Alistair sing had been, ages ago. That same thrill, that same sensation that she was witnessing an artist basking in his element, effortlessly commanding the thoughts and feelings of his audience. At one point she had looked Alistair up—it wasn't like he'd ever contacted her again—and found that he had come to absolutely nothing at all.

A small, nasty glimmer of satisfaction at that.

2022 began to roll slowly into view, its shape vaguely visible over the top of a hill. The weather turned cool and then almost cold for a moment, but then back to cool again. Tessa had put her heaviest coat in the closet last year, but she was beginning to understand that she wouldn't need it this winter. Maybe she would never need it again.

On New Year's Eve, she and Jupiter went to a party. Pearl was also invited, but she said she had to attend a cooking class. "You sure?" Jupiter pressed. "We'll only see the dawn of 2022 once."

"I'm good. Have fun, guys." Pearl turned back to the sink, where she was washing a knife. But Tessa caught the hint of a smile, and the two of them questioned her until she admitted that the cooking class was more of a New Year's party, and it would probably include at least as much drinking as cooking. "Hopefully we don't all get blasted and accidentally gut each other with our filleting knives."

That evening, Tessa borrowed Pearl's fishnet top and paired it with her own leather pants. Jupiter wore an all-silver outfit and his new handmade crown. He had fashioned it himself out of wire, so that it formed a kind of bird-cage around his skull, similar to what Tessa imagined the first crowns had looked like: tangles of branches with the thorns cut off.

They made their way to the party. It was nearly seventy degrees, although it was already dark. She was sweating as she walked, a light sheen making its way down her back and along her arms, sticking her legs to her pants. The wrongness of this felt immense. It was so warm she could almost pretend it was summer in New York. It certainly felt nothing like the winters she remembered as a child, which had never been snowy the way they were in Manhattan, but had also not been *seventy degrees*.

They arrived at the party just before midnight. They got drinks and found a spot near the stage, where a DJ was clearly playing the most upbeat, energetic tunes he could think of. The venue was large and echoing, a space like a hollowed-out cube. Lights marched back and forth on the walls, blinking on and off, illuminating their faces in turns: faded underwater blue, forest green, magnificent purple. Jupiter had recently removed the bandages from his newest tattoo, a big one on his right bicep, and now it stood out in stark detail: a snake curling in a perfect circle, devouring itself. The scales near its neck were detailed and realistic but faded near its tail, growing segmented, wormlike, abstract. Its single eye winked at Tessa in the stuttering light.

She thought of the last club she had played in with her old band, nearly a decade ago. It had been a big open box like this, full of lights, but with much bigger windows. What had it been called? Snot Glass? Jesus, no. *Shot* Glass. That place had been so strange. A big lit-up square in a no-name town in the middle of the desert. She could still remember the way the air had tasted, dusty and hot, and the surreal feeling of the town, atmosphere like an ominous fever dream. Although maybe that was just her interpretation of it now. Maybe she was warping her own memories, pasting over them with what had happened afterwards.

"Where am I going to get my New Year's kiss?" Jupiter was saying, looking around. "Time's running out."

"Time's running out for me too," she said, still thinking of the Shot Glass. "We're both nearly thirty." Maybe if she spent less time looking up Methuselah and more time looking up single men, she would have a New Year's kiss herself.

"Oh my god, Tessa, I meant for tonight, as in, it's nearly midnight. I didn't ask to be *attacked*."

"Ha ha, sorry. Look, what about that guy?" She pointed to a slender, effeminate man with eyeliner smudged around his lashes.

"He literally has a girlfriend."

"Oh." Tessa looked more closely, and just at that moment, the girl next to the man pulled him in for a long, tongue-twining kiss.

"See? These days you can't even tell who's gay or straight anymore. There's plenty of options for you, though. What about him? He looks large and in charge." He indicated a tall, broadly built man a few feet to their left. After gathering her courage, Tessa sidled over and tapped the man on the shoulder, but when he turned to look at her she saw instantly that he wasn't into her. There was a distanced politeness in his eyes, and he didn't even blink as she aborted her first attempts at conversation and melted back into the crowd.

"No luck?"

"Nah."

"Sorry. He's an idiot. Clearly. He knows you're out of

his league. I just pointed him out so he could see what a beautiful girl he *doesn't* get to kiss."

She forced herself to laugh.

A minute later, the countdown began. The two of them looked at each other. She had never noticed before how his hair was even longer than Alistair's had been, although it was platinum, not dark. She wondered where Alistair was now. He had probably cut all his hair off and started working at some corporate firm.

Jupiter shrugged and pulled Tessa in for a kiss. For half a second she expected it to feel like kissing a girl, which she had done in college a few times; their mouths had been so small, their lips unpleasantly delicate. But of course it didn't feel like that. Jupiter was gay, but he was still a man, and his mouth felt like any other man's mouth. He pulled away as soon as the "Happy New Year!" was over, and she stood there, her body as jolted as if an electric current had been run through it.

"Welcome to 2022," he said, and she smiled back, her ears already hurting from the cacophony around them. Her blood pulsed insistent in her veins, thudding thick and heavy and powerful from one end of her body to the other. "It'll be a year of greatness, don't you think?"

When they got back to the apartment, Pearl had returned from her cooking class. For a second Tessa thought Jupiter might mention the kiss to Pearl, but of course he didn't. He told Pearl they'd had a great time and asked her how her cooking class-slash-party had gone.

"It was amazing," Pearl burbled. "This guy Ryan asked me to be his cooking partner."

Jupiter whistled. "Ooh, cooking partner. That sounds serious. Is that like a pre-engagement step?"

Instead of coming back with a sarcastic retort, Pearl just

giggled and shrugged. Tessa believed she was witnessing the first stages of romantic infatuation, and she also believed that it wasn't really anything anybody should be seeing, so she went into her room. Her head was blurry; she could still hear the echoes of the music from the party bouncing around her skull. Could still hear the sounds of the fireworks outside, spattering hot against the night.

CHAPTER FIVE

BARSTOW, CALIFORNIA, 2014

At night in the motel, Tessa checked her messages. There was one from her friend Emma, saying: *How's the road going?? Have you met any hot male groupies yet?* 

She thought of Alistair and felt a flash of heat, a dip in her stomach. Right now their room was quiet. Alistair was sleeping in his bed, early for him—it was only eleven—but they'd decided not to hang out as a group tonight. Once he'd shared the news about booking the Shot Glass, there had seemed to be no more point in remaining sequestered closely together. It got to be too much, the lack of space, and sometimes Tessa felt that she was going to start yelling at everyone to get the fuck out.

She began to type a response, but hesitated halfway through, even though she knew that if Emma was online she could see the three dots that symbolized her typing. She'd begun to write, *No hot male groupies so far, I think the guys are scaring them all away :(* but didn't have the heart to click Send.

The truth was, Emma, like many other people from

Tessa's past, thought they were a lot more successful than they really were. For most people, people who didn't really follow music, the band's Instagram and Facebook posts were their only measure of success. To the untrained eye, as long as everything looked fine on those fronts, they seemed to be doing well. Of the members, Tessa was the best with social media and photography, and she was the one who took most of the behind-the-scenes snaps of the band: Emrys on the drums, the sinewy muscles in his arms standing out. Alistair warming up behind the mic, his throat lean and erotic enough to send a pulse of heat through Tessa's stomach. Nico's face twisted in concentration on the bass, Zac on his guitar. She uploaded these pictures onto Instagram and Facebook with vague, tantalizing captions such as *Getting ready for the next big thing!* Or *Something to look out for come next fall...* By the time next fall came, she would go back and delete these captions, leaving only the picture, not that anyone probably cared enough to go back and look and say, "Hey, it's September—wasn't Pestilential Harbor supposed to be giving us the Next Big Thing right about now?"

A lot of the people who liked their posts were former classmates of Tessa and Emrys, people they'd gone to high school with who had ended up studying law at Stanford or computer science at MIT or business at Yale. These people only knew of the band's existence via social media, seeing everything through an oversaturated, cropped, halogen-tinted light. This meant they had no way of knowing what it was really like for the band—they didn't follow the band as they slouched from city to city in Nico's RV that already had rust streaking down the sides, didn't sit next to them in diners and Burger Kings as they squabbled about song titles and expenses. They weren't with them in the Barstow supermarket the other night as Emrys and Zac argued over the price of Talenti ice cream versus Ben and Jerry's. ("It's almost double the price!" Zac had exclaimed. "Are you insane?" "The quality makes up for it," Emrys argued, and staunchly maintained that its higher-quality ingredients made it far less unhealthy and more satisfying than Ben and Jerry's. In the end, Zac had won.)

They didn't know what a failure Pestilential Harbor had turned out to be. Although sometimes Tessa wondered if they had guessed. For one thing, there was a conspicuous lack of video lately on the band's pages, and though she recycled recordings of old shows, if someone looked closely enough it would be impossible not to notice. Maybe the likes were ironic, pitying. Maybe when Angelica from high school (currently at Fordham, planning to pursue a medical degree) commented *Amazing! You guys ROCK* underneath a photo of the band, she could tell it was recycled from one of their shows last summer, and she knew they were a failure, was talking to her new future doctor friends about it and saying how relieved she was not to have done anything as stupid as to try to join a metal band right out of high school.

Tessa put her phone down, closed her eyes and dug her knuckles into the sockets. Stars bloomed in the darkness, tiny white specks against the reddish black, whole galaxies expanding and dying in her mind.

She knew it was stupid to worry this much about a social media page when there was the band's *actual* success to worry about. Actual venues to book and money that was running out. But often social media did feel more real than the real thing. Unlike real life, you could look at it, zoom in on it, measure it and categorize it and, if you wanted, print it out on a glossy sixteen-by-twelve sheet of paper and hang it on your bedroom wall. You couldn't do that with anything that was, supposedly, *real*.

Tessa glanced over at the still-sleeping figure of Alistair. She wished he could tolerate her body in his bed, that she could sleep with him. They did cuddle together after sex, but only for a few minutes. She had never had the experience of lying with him for long hours, their limbs tangled up, drifting in and out of the pools of unconsciousness.

She put her phone, with the half-answered text from Emma, down on the table as softly as she could—Alistair was a light sleeper—and crept out of their room to get a snack from the vending machine down the hall. The motel hallway was long and murkily lit. The vending machine hummed and glowed at the end of the corridor, ceaselessly. The light emanating from it was as artificial as any she could imagine: the glow of civilizations on distant planets, of stations deep under the sea. She had the feeling that society could collapse and the world descend into barbarism, and still the vending machine would keep on humming and glowing at the end of the corridor, powered by some internal fuel source.

She scanned the options. There were soft-baked cookies and Oreos and sour candy, and they caught her eye first, pulling her in with their bright colors and promise of an energy spike. But she knew that if she bought any of these, she might go back to the vending machine over and over again and eat sugar for hours, her hand moving from the bags to her mouth in an unceasing cycle. She'd wake up with a gritty taste in her mouth and dull nausea in her stomach. She used to eat too much sugar and the habit was still there, deep down, a junkie's craving that had never quite gone away.

A memory from five years ago came back to her, from

when she had gone to see her dad for the weekend. She'd been fourteen and fat, switching from iPod to iPhone to iPad, eating junk food continuously and whining about how sick she felt. She remembered her father looking into the refrigerator and then closing it with a tight slap. "Why do I feel sick?" she'd asked him.

"I don't know." In her memory his face was long and disapproving. "Maybe because you eat nothing but candy. Maybe because you spend all day on those devices of yours."

"Sorry you grew up without electricity," she said sarcastically.

"Your grandmother, you know, actually did grow up without electricity."

"Yeah, and see how she turned out."

He rounded on her. "What did you say?"

The scene looped over and over again in her memory. The bratty, nasty tone of her voice, like something slinking out from beneath the sofa; the cold bilious feeling in her stomach. She remembered how after that conversation, for the rest of the night, she ate nothing but chocolate, even though it began to taste wrong, disgusting: undertones of ketchup, barbecue sauce, processed meat. She kept putting more of it in her mouth even though she felt sicker with each bite, because she didn't know how to stop. Her father in the other room, reading or working, virtuous without his devices. She ate more and more chocolate until the smell made her gag. The definition of insanity was doing the same thing over and over again and expecting different results. The definition of insanity was doing the same thing forever.

Now, standing in the motel hallway, Tessa selected a bag of chips. Half a second too late, she realized that she should have chosen something less audibly crunchy—now she would have to eat them slowly, letting each one dissolve on her tongue before being able to chew it.

Walking back, she heard a spill of voices from the room next door. She knew she should continue back to her room and not eavesdrop, but they were all members of the band. It wasn't like Nico and Emrys and Zac were shacking up next door all romantic like she and Alistair were. And they seemed to be discussing something that was pertinent to the band's future—she caught the words *gigs* and *money* and *band*.

"That's exactly what I'm saying," Nico said. "It's been bad ever since then."

"Well, what do you think he's trying to do? This could be really good for us. I'm glad someone's taken initiative." That was Zac.

"And is it even going to help, or are we just gonna keep spiraling down despite this?"

"We should've cut her after all." Soft voice: this was Emrys.

She froze, trying to breathe as gently as possible, even though there was no way they'd hear her. Surely they were talking about someone else, she thought frantically, even though there was only one *her* in the band (or pretty much anyone the band knew).

"I *told* you guys," Emrys continued. "She's dead weight."

"Maybe you were right." This: Zac.

A coldness spread over Tessa. So they had all decided the same thing about her. She was dead weight to them. *Dead weight?* Her vocals were, maybe not incredible, but definitely at least good. She was a talented soprano, and she could dip into the alto range, too—not that it was usually necessary, with Alistair there to sing alongside her.

Maybe she should knock on the door, say something. But she couldn't see the point of confronting them. It wouldn't change their minds about cutting her. If they all got together and decided to kick her out, she wouldn't be able to do anything about it.

Zac, she didn't know so well. And Nico had always been kind of a wild card. But *Emrys*? What had she ever done to him? They'd always been cool. It was true that they'd floated somewhere in between friends and acquaintances in their freshman and sophomore years, the sort of people who sat together at lunch for company but didn't really say much to each other. But in the last two years of high school, something had shifted, and—as if suddenly realizing that they would all be leaving one another shortly —the up-to-that-point loose cliques had begun shrinking, forming much more tightly-knit groups. And one such group that formed was Tessa and Emrys and Emma and Madison—and occasionally Nico, who could always be counted upon to provide weed and alcohol.

Tessa had always seen Emrys as something of an artistic misfit, like herself. He was poetic and often melodramatic, and sometimes she thought he took the band a bit too seriously. Not the band itself, exactly, but parts of what they were doing. He obsessed over certain trivial details, like these things would make all the difference in their success— agonizing for hours over a word choice in the least important verse of a song, or insisting on changing a song title several times.

Or, apparently, deciding that their female singer was extraneous.

She went back into her room, not bothering to close the door quietly. Alistair groaned. "Can you please be quieter," he said. His voice was fuzzy with sleep.

"So you wanted to cut me."

"Huh? Tessa, what's going on? I was sleeping."

"Well, nobody else is." She tossed the chips onto the table. "They're all next door discussing whether I should be kicked out of the band. But I guess you already know about this? Emrys pretty much made it clear that he told everyone. Well—everyone besides me." She hated how her voice was shaking.

Alistair said nothing, only sat up fully in bed.

She sat down on her own bed, head in her hands. Thin, bitter liquid was filling her stomach. She wasn't hungry anymore; she'd better throw the chips away.

All of them, all of them were against her. And Emrys— she could barely believe it, but it sounded like it had been his idea. Fucking Emrys. With all his talk about how he *embodied the gentle side of death*: what a pathetic attempt at being deep, what a deceitful veneer he had pasted up over his true nature. She'd known him since ninth grade, explained the finer workings of calculus to him, and this was how he repaid her? By suggesting she be kicked out of the band she had started?

"Tessa," Alistair said. "Tessa, listen to me."

She snorted. The sound was harsh to her own ears. "Oh, great. Don't tell me you suggested it in the first place. Although I wouldn't be surprised—Emrys always did seem like too much of a wuss to come up with even one really mean idea on his own."

"I promise you I didn't. But yeah, there was a time, a few weeks ago, where he did say something like that."

"Mhmm."

He threw off the covers and sat on the edge of the bed. His bare feet were slim, vulnerable-looking in the moon- light. "He was being pretty stupid. He said something like, maybe you're the reason we haven't been able to book anything. Maybe people don't want to see a metal band with a female singer."

"That's garbage. What about Nightwish? Within Temptation? Leaves' Eyes?"

"Plus he said that we already have a male singer, so—"

"Great. Yeah, you don't even need to make the effort of finding another singer. You can just step up and replace me."

"Tessa! I said no. I said he was being an idiot, that he was going too far. Our vocals work well together, we harmonize great—it's a big part of the band's identity."

"And the others? What did they say?"

"Well. You know Zac, he goes along with whoever seems to be winning the argument. And Nico was too busy grumbling about his mom cutting off his allowance—"

"*What?*"

Alistair sucked in a breath. He had the face of someone who has said something they definitely should not have.

"What's this about cutting off his allowance?" So this was why he'd said all that stuff back at the diner, about money running out. She thought back: had the others' faces been more serious than hers, had they understood something she hadn't been privy to?

"She's not cutting it off yet," Alistair finally said. "But she said...maybe when he turns twenty-three."

"Jesus, why did nobody tell me?"

"We didn't want to worry you."

"What am I, just the pretty singer? I don't get to be a part of the band's discussions? I founded it. Well, me and Nico and Emrys. Although I don't think they should count right about now, as they want to fucking throw me out."

At this, Alistair's face darkened. "We're all members of the band. Each one of us is just as important as any other."

"Clearly not, as four-fifths of the band is having discussions about throwing the remaining twenty percent out on her ass."

"We're not. Emrys brought that up a few weeks ago, I shut him down, and everyone seemed to be on the same page after that. We're not kicking anyone out."

She shrugged. "That's not what they're saying next door." The two of them seemed to be going around in circles. She looked down at the stripe of moonlight on the floor again, and realized it wasn't moonlight at all: it was the artificial glow from the streetlights next to the road. Of course. Moonlight could not exist in a place like this. There was no real nature here. Their band was living in an artificial bubble: false moonlight, false camaraderie, false friendship and respect.

"What did you hear?"

"Well, I didn't exactly press my ear to the door, but I heard...enough. Emrys was saying that he *told* them to kick me out, and called me dead weight, then Nico was like, *It's been bad ever since then,* or maybe he said that before, I don't know, oh and then Zac said it's good someone like Emrys is taking initiative—so at least someone's being appreciated around here. God, I want to go in there and tell them how fucking fake they are."

"I don't blame you."

"Why didn't you tell them that?" she demanded.

"I told him he was being an idiot."

"I think he needs to hear something a little stronger than that."

"Maybe you're right. But promise me, don't say

anything until after this show. We need to be united for it, okay? I don't want this to jeopardize us."

She let out a breath. "How can I work with them knowing how they feel about me?"

He opened his mouth, closed it again, and sighed. "Once we get that venue, we'll be on the upswing. Just promise me you won't say anything until then, okay?"

She looked away.

"Okay?"

"Okay, geez, fine."

"Come here," he said.

"I thought you couldn't sleep with someone else in your bed."

"I wasn't thinking about sleeping."

On top of him, she could see the contours of his face in the room's fake lunar glow. The crooked path of his nose. The shape of his mouth as he said her name, but quietly, so that the sound would remain contained within the room's walls.

A while later, she asked: "Do you miss home?" Their breathing was the only sound in the room. She couldn't make out any noises from next door; the others might have gone to sleep by now.

"Not really."

She didn't know much about Alistair's home life except that he was one of four siblings: two brothers, one sister. It was rare that families were so big nowadays, and she'd asked him question after question about what it was like to grow up surrounded by your peers.

Now, she wondered how it was possible that Alistair

didn't miss home. She missed everything. She missed walking out into the living room in the morning on the weekends and finding her mother doing her yoga there, ascetic on her mat, her hair turning honey-golden in the light. She missed the In-N-Out Burger near her school, the skating rink she used to go to before she got too busy. She even missed the classrooms of her high school, the scent of pencil shavings and binders and library books with their smudged, peeling spines. She missed everywhere she had ever been, all her life, simply because it represented the past which she could not get back.

And yet she did not want to turn tail and slink back to San Jose; did not want to admit that she had failed, that she had been wrong.

She told Alistair this, mumbling it into the warm stretch of skin between his shoulder and armpit, unable to look him in the eye as she confessed her cowardice. "Do you ever miss the past," she said, "just because it represents somewhere you can't go back to?"

"Never." He sounded genuinely confused. "Why would I want to go back?"

She couldn't think of a reply to this. "Why not?" she fumbled.

"We're only nineteen years old. I'll be twenty soon. We're at the very beginnings of our lives. What would you even go back to—diapers and nap time?"

"Well, the past is unchangeable," she began. But at this he only looked more confused, and she knew she wouldn't be able to explain, so she said "Never mind" and changed the subject.

It wasn't that she was longing for the comforts of childhood and home and having someone to take care of her. It wasn't even that. It was more like: the past was above all else something you could never get back to, and that was what made it so hypnotizing. Even if you revisited an old room, made everything exactly the same—wore the same clothes you'd worn four years ago, listened to the same music, smelled the same scents—it would not be the same. Because you, and the world outside the room, were no longer the same. Your life kept unreeling, moving in one direction only. The past was ungraspable by its very definition, flickering forever out of reach.

Around 2 a.m., Tessa ended up sending a short reply to Emma, saying,

> No groupies yet, but I'll let you know when
> they show up !

There was an extra space in between *up* and the exclamation point, but she left it there, because it would add to the illusion that she was in a rush when sending the text, caught in between too many important things to bother checking it for small mistakes. She was industrious, bustling, significant. She had a future.

CHAPTER SIX

SAN DIEGO, CALIFORNIA, 2022

Tessa's New Year's kiss with Jupiter should not have made such an impression upon her, but it did. It had been years since she had been in a relationship. She was about to turn twenty-eight, and shamefully, her last actual relationship had been in college. It had been a bland, dull relationship, echoing the mindless boredom of her classes, and she'd ended it immediately upon graduation, as though she were being timed. Over the last few years she'd bounced from dating app to dating app, a slave to both her libido and her need for affection—they seemed to be wholly separate things—bringing guys home every once in a while, going back to their places more often. Most of these guys turned out to be rude or awkward or creepy and she never wanted to see them again.

There were guys she liked, of course. There was the software developer who stopped answering her texts but continued watching and reacting to every post she put on social media. There was the guy who kept saying he wanted to see her, but conjured an ungodly array of ailments whenever she asked him out. There were more but they blended together, just an assortment of names and smiles and hands and dicks, none more remarkable than any other in the end.

For the next few days, Tessa could not look at Jupiter without remembering how his mouth had felt on hers. The way the room had exploded around them, energy and noise erupting through the air. The lust humming through her body like electricity coming down a wire. She found it difficult to maintain eye contact with him, and whenever the three of them would group on the sofa to watch TV or sit at the table to eat one of Pearl's home-cooked meals, she would consciously choose not to sit next to him. Whenever she got too close to him that buzzing would come back, that energy that made her feel like her body had been cracked open.

It was true that from what she knew, Jupiter identified as gay. At least, he'd only ever mentioned being with guys. But these days, people weren't always so strictly bound to one side or the other. It wasn't necessarily a dichotomy. He'd kissed her, so that meant something, didn't it? Those girls who were disgusted by the idea of kissing another woman, who would never, *ever* do it—surely they were more straight than Jupiter was gay. And if he'd kissed her, who knew what else he was willing to experiment with. She kept thinking about the celebrities who had recently come out as pansexual, their attraction not restricted to one gender or another but unrelated to such things. Surpassing such things.

One evening in mid-January, Tessa found Jupiter hard at work on the computer in the dining room. He was running his hands through his hair; she felt hot looking at them, their thick knuckles and prominent veins and blocky fingers. She imagined those hands on her.

He glanced up and saw that she was staring at him. "Hey," he said.

"Hey. How's it going? You look busy."

"Unfortunately. It's bloody hard work."

"You need to work on your accent." She came over to the table. "You sounded Australian there for a second."

"You think that's Australian? Sheila, you want Australian? I'll give you Australian! Throw some shrimp on the barbie, roight, and—" He began ranting in a near-unintelligible mix of Australian and Cockney. "G'day mate! I can't Adam and Eve it!"

She doubled over with laughter. "Jupiter, are you okay? Do I need to call an ambulance?"

He sighed. "No, I'm afraid they might actually take me away and lock me up somewhere. It's just this bloody project. I need to de-stress."

"What do you think would help you de-stress?"

"A drink, for one." He leaned back in his chair, laced his arms over his head, stretching so far his ribs threatened to poke through his stomach. His shirt hiked up, exposing a thin sliver of stomach above the waistband of his jeans. Tessa dragged her eyes away. "Maybe two."

"Maybe a massage?" she suggested.

"Maybe."

She said it before she even ran the words through her mind, before she even thought how they'd sound: "Or...we could kiss again."

She'd meant it to sound flirty, but she sounded like a six-year-old. *We could kiss again.* Her body prickled and burned with shame.

A moment of silence. Then: "Tessa," he said gently. "You know I'm gay."

"Yeah. Of course. I was just wondering if—I mean, sexuality is a scale—"

"Yup. Kinsey, I know all about it. But I'm pretty much

as firmly on the gay side as it's possible to be." More silence. "Uh, sorry if I gave you the wrong impression the other night. I really wanted my New Year's Kiss, and I guess I just got a bit carried away."

There seemed nothing more to say after this. The awkwardness was taking its own shape in the air, sucking up all the oxygen. "Sorry," she managed. "It was, um, a stupid suggestion. I just figured since we did it once, we could do it again, ha ha, but clearly it was just a one-time thing…"

She couldn't stop babbling. She suddenly became aware of the language she was using, how it could come off as pushy or manipulative, and she added, "That's totally fine, though, I don't care. Don't feel pressured, please, forget I said anything."

He laughed, but he sounded uncomfortable too. *I've ruined everything,* she thought in despair. *I've ruined everything.* "You should get busier on those apps, Tessa. It's beginning to feel like *Flowers in the Attic* or something in here. Have you tried this new app called Chemystery? Like chemistry and mystery. It's like Tinder, but with all these personality quizzes. Some of them go pretty deep, too."

"Sounds cool!" she forced out. "I'll look into it." Then she babbled something about not having a lot of time lately, and adding that perhaps it was this that had led her to make such a stupid suggestion, to be so silly and thoughtless. Her face bloomed with heat; she was so embarrassed she could barely see. The next moment she had fled into her room, where she screamed into a pillow until she had no more breath left at all.

Now it was Jupiter's turn to avoid Tessa's eyes. He avoided her presence, too; she noticed that when she came out into the living room to work, he was never there. He worked in his room more often now, like he was scared of her. She tried to apologize again, when he was on his way out of the shower (horrible time to speak to him, really, but they'd run into each other in the hall and she had to say *something*) but he interrupted her, saying there was nothing to apologize for, that she was being silly, don't worry about it, and what did she think of Pearl's couscous salad they'd had for lunch?

But still. He avoided looking her in the eyes. Another thing that had changed: he stopped bringing guys home. Now he went over to their places instead, and she knew he meant it as a courtesy to her, but every time he disappeared in the evening she sat in a knot at her computer, her brain a chamber ringing with guilt. She ran over her words, replaying every hideous detail of that night and the days that had followed, leading up to the final suggestion that they *kiss again.* How stupid, how blind she had been.

What's wrong with me? she thought. *Why do I continually chase men that don't like me back?* Or, sometimes— *What's wrong with me that they don't like me back?* Although this last was not something she thought when it came to Jupiter. The answer was simple: she was not a man. Although—maybe even if she *were* a man, maybe Jupiter still wouldn't want her. This thought, too, tormented her, led her down murky hallways of thought where she began wondering if there was simply something intrinsic about *her* that was wrong.

No, she thought at these times. *There's nothing about me that's wrong.* She tried to convince herself: *I'm in my twenties, I've got a waist-to-hip ratio like the curve of a double bass, I'm lush and beautiful and young.*

One night, after Jupiter had left on yet another date, she turned on her glow-lamp, switched it to the blue setting so that the bedroom was filled with a cool arctic light. She did her eyeliner, flicking it up into perfect triangular wings, a skill that had always come to her without effort. She put on her favorite music—Purity Ring, Flor—and for a while she *was* lush and young and beautiful as she lay on her bed, gazing slit-eyed at the ceiling, quietly singing along. The lyrics of these songs were so much less literal than those she had sung for Pestilential Harbor, so much vaguer and more malleable. She could interpret them any way she wanted: something that was fine to do with lyrics, but definitely not with people. Doing that with Jupiter—trying to glimpse, in his queerness, an opening for herself—had been her mistake.

The music switched to *silkspun*, a song whose lyrics Tessa had never even been able to half-decipher. She lost herself in their unknowability, while all around her the ceiling and walls shone azure and strange. She imagined that she was inside a glacier. Held inside its perfect, other-worldly glow. The transcendent feeling this created—the sensation that she was not in an apartment at all, but in the frozen, centuries-old, anonymous heart of the world—was oddly comforting. When she grew tired, she turned the music and the light off and snuggled beneath her blankets.

But the next day she awoke with her eyeliner smudged and her throat sore, and by lunchtime she realized that Jupiter was still gone, and the day continued on with his absence pressing on her like a finger on a bruise.

Pearl saw that she was upset, but had no idea what it was about. "Guy trouble?" she suggested at one point. By now it was evening, muggy, with rain coming down outside: huge warm droplets the size of coins splashing onto the streets, darkening the pavement and running into each other like her mother's freckles. At the thought of her mother Tessa felt a pull of longing—and then, immediately following it, disgust. She was close to thirty years old. She had no right to be longing for her mommy.

"Something like that." Tessa didn't say anything more, simply let her roommate imagine that it was a heterosexual male she was longing for, in a healthy and uncomplicated manner, rather than their eccentric gay roommate. Their gay roommate who was probably at this very moment having sex with another guy. She stifled a laugh and looked at the rain streaking down the window.

"Do you want some food?"

Pearl offered people food whenever they seemed the slightest bit upset. They could be undergoing anything from the death of a relative to a few extra hours of work, and she would suggest food as a remedy. The strangest thing was that it worked. Her food really did help everyone feel better. Once Jupiter had suggested that Pearl was a spirit from another world, that she was part of a tribe of sprites who lured hungry travelers into the forest with the phantom scents of meals, and then devoured them. Pearl had giggled, holding her tiny hand to her mouth. "I'm not a murderous food spirit!"

"That's exactly what a murderous food spirit would say," Jupiter had replied.

This exchange, all the talk about spirits luring men to their deaths, had made Tessa think of Siren's Lament, and she'd found, with some sadness, that she could no longer recall the melody.

"Sure," Tessa said now. "If it's not a lot of trouble. Did you already make something?"

"No—and that's the best part." Pearl's face lit up, and she headed for the kitchen.

"Don't go to any trouble. Don't make something just for me!"

"Sit back down," Pearl called. "I was going to cook anyway. You're not the only ones who get hungry around here."

The reference to Jupiter, even though it was off-center and sideways, hardly mentioning him at all, made Tessa sink back into her chair.

Pearl made Chicken Tikka Masala and glazed carrots with coriander. They ate in silence, broken only by Tessa telling her how good the food was. The sauce was rich and creamy, with just the right amount of spices.

"You'd be a great mom," Tessa said, and for a moment Pearl looked surprised, and she thought she had, once again, said something wrong.

But then Pearl beamed. "I hope so. *My* children aren't going to be picky eaters, those annoying kids who refuse to eat anything other than Wonder Bread and sour candy. They're going to have their palates exposed to a wide array of food by the time they turn four years old." A pause, and then: "Do you think you'll ever have children?" There was something shrewd in Pearl's expression that Tessa did not quite like.

"I don't know," Tessa said. "I don't think so. I hope not."

"Those are three very different answers."

"Well, no offense, but..."

"Slow down with the *no offense*. I'm not a mom *yet*." Pearl laughed.

"I guess, no offense to you, as someone who wants children? But I can't even imagine being pregnant or giving birth. I also can't really get behind the idea of bringing someone new into this world. I mean, with how things are going—whole parts of the Southwest are going to be unlivable. We hit 130 degrees in Death Valley last summer. We're in the middle of a two-decade mega-drought. Millions and millions of acres of forest are being destroyed, beautiful ancient trees that withstood centuries of weather and change up until now. And that's just the area around here."

Tessa abruptly realized how fast she was speaking and how wide Pearl's eyes were. *Better slow down before you start talking about Methuselah.* "Anyway. I don't really feel like it's my place to bring a child into the world, not right now, and probably not ever."

There was another reason, too, something she had never admitted to anyone: she was not sure if she would love her child the way she was supposed to. What if she gave birth to it and the nurse handed it to her, all sticky and slimed in red juices, and she saw it not as her angel or her miracle but instead as what it actually was: a lump of flesh, barely seeing or hearing, just screaming and shitting and screaming. What if she thought, *Ew. Get this thing away from me.*

And then what? Then what would she do? She couldn't just *return* it.

"But don't listen to me," Tessa said. "Again, I'm sure you'll be a great mom."

Pearl ran a hand through her hair. "Thanks," she said. "I think you would be too." But there was something unconvincing in Pearl's tone, and Tessa put another forkful of food in her mouth so she wouldn't have to reply.

When she was in her room later, scrolling her newsfeeds in an attempt to lull her brain into sleep, she heard the front door close. It was nearly 1 a.m. After almost twenty-four hours, Jupiter was back. Pearl was still in the living room, and Tessa heard her exclaim at his late return, asking him how his date had gone. She was loud, excited, not bothering to lower her voice—why would she? But Jupiter did lower his voice, and Tessa didn't hear his reply.

2022 turned out to be a year of greatness after all: greater fires, greater droughts, greater unemployment. Every time there was a fire, Tessa checked the status of Methuselah—frantically, obsessively. Sometimes she even had thoughts of visiting the Inyo National Forest and tracking it down herself. An insane idea: Inyo National Forest spanned two million acres. She could hike across it for weeks—stumbling, dehydrated, hopelessly lost—and never find the tree. And even if she did stumble across it, she was so used to staring at pictures of it on a screen, at the living being crushed into two-dimensional pixels, who was to say whether she would recognize it at all.

By the end of 2022, Pearl had moved out of the apartment to live with Ryan, the guy she'd met at her cooking class. In the middle of 2023, Jupiter moved out as well, although he didn't mention if he was going to be living with someone else or not. After that one evening, they had never again spoken of the kiss they shared.

At least Tessa could afford the apartment by herself now. Walking around it was like walking around a graveyard—but it was more of a graveyard for herself, because while her former roommates had grown up and moved out and at least one of them was cohabiting with a partner, she had remained the same. Still in the same job, still single, still taking the same antidepressants every morning. Once or twice she considered moving, but then one day she opened a cupboard she almost never used and found a package of safety pins with one missing. *Jupiter's homemade ear piercing!* If she moved, she thought, maybe the memories would vanish as well. They weren't great, but they were all she had.

Tessa went to New York to visit her father every so often, and they, too, went to the Bronx to visit his mother every so often. Tessa's grandmother still refused to move out and allow Carl to buy her a better apartment. She was now ninety-four years old, cadaverous, the outline of her skull visible beneath her skin. The skin itself looked like thin layers of silk clinging to the bones. Her hands were pale, emaciated birds. Carl had gotten her a live-in nurse, and Tessa remembered how she had once refused this, maintaining proudly that even at ninety-one she could look after herself. Now she did not even seem to notice the nurse's presence. The nurse was a plump forty-something woman from Jamaica, and quietly slipped in and out of the room to hand Grise cups of water and clean up the dishes in the sink.

Grise did not teach Tessa any more German, or make any more snappy comments about her work schedule. Instead she rambled from one topic to the next; her sentences were long and meandering, like a traveler that had gotten lost on the road and now kept retracing their steps in the gathering darkness. She told stories about her childhood, and then told Carl how proud she was of him, and then told Tessa how beautiful she was. Then she looped back to her childhood, sometimes slipping into a rough, blocky language that Tessa recognized as German, although she had no idea what her grandmother was saying.

Every few minutes, she would say this: "I want to go home."

Tessa thought that even if she herself lived to be ninety-four years old, she would never forget those words. Nor the lost, confused tone in which they were spoken.

"You are home, Mom," Carl would reply, but she'd shake her head.

Tessa knew Carl wanted to force his mother into a hospital, but when he brought up "assisted living," Grise began crying. Tessa suspected that it was more the tone of Carl's voice—coaxing, placatory, full of manufactured comfort—when he said those words that alarmed her, rather than the words themselves. And upon seeing his mother's tears, Carl's face took on a look of helplessness that Tessa had never seen before.

Tessa counted down the minutes until they could leave.

Finally Tessa and Carl were outside again, walking back to his apartment. The streetlights cast long shadows between the cars. If Tessa relaxed her eyes, they looked bottomless, like trenches gouged in the earth. It was late, and she needed to wake up early in two days to fly back to San Diego, but she didn't intend on sleeping anytime soon; she didn't want to leave her father alone. There was still that helpless expression on his face.

It was only when they got back to the apartment that Tessa realized she hadn't seen a single tree the whole time they'd been walking. Maybe she just hadn't been looking. Or maybe the trees really had grown so thin, so stunted—

the way she'd predicted, years before—that they had simply blended into the background, vanished from her line of sight.

"Would you like to see what Grandma was like when she was younger?" Carl asked, apropos of nothing.

"Sure," Tessa said, her mind still on the vanishing trees.

He took a book down from a high shelf in the closet. "This is her old yearbook—she gave it to me when we were cleaning out the apartment, after my dad died." It was a deep red, and when he opened it the pages reacted stiffly, sticking to each other. "It's seventy years old," he said by way of explanation.

Tessa brushed her fingers over the first pages. They were thick and yellowish, giving off a smell like resin, like sap.

"Here," he said. He turned to the point where the book fell open easily, the page it had been opened to again and again. Here there was a spread of girls, six of them on each page, two in each row. "This is your grandmother when she was twenty-one years old." He pointed to the top row.

"Oh my god, she's *gorgeous*," Tessa said reflexively. The boldness of her statement embarrassed her at first, but it was true—even by today's standards, she was stunning. Especially by today's standards. She looked a little like Ariana Grande, with her sharp cheekbones and precisely defined jawline. She had dark liquid eyes, and her gaze was cast slightly upward, towards the edge of the frame, as though someone over there had just called her name. Her nose was slim and defined, and below it, plump lips shone with lipstick that Tessa knew was probably red but looked black in the picture. She reminded Tessa of alternative models, the ones who wore purple lipstick and combat boots and leather jackets. Her eyes held a blend of emotions; there was a vulnerability to her stare, but there was startled wisdom too, as though she had only recently become conscious of her own shattering beauty.

"Really? You think so?" His eyes crinkled, and he looked from Tessa to the picture with tenderness. She could tell that he was pleased.

"Yeah, of course! Is that a real fur coat?"

He looked at the picture for a few moments, and Tessa saw his expression change. "That's not her," he said eventually. "The girl on the right, that's my mother."

"Oh." She clapped a hand to her mouth. "Oh my god, sorry!" And sure enough, there were their names: Rachel Merritt on the left, Grise Seidel on the right. She hadn't even looked at the names below their images; she'd just glanced automatically at the more beautiful one. What kind of shallow person was she?

The woman in the right picture looked much more like her grandmother, and she questioned how she could have ever thought the girl on the left was her. Her hair and eye color were admittedly the same, but besides that, not a single feature matched. Her grandmother's nose, for one thing—it had always been big, and the girl on the right had a broad, bulbous nose, although in the picture it was a bit smaller than Tessa remembered it being. And her eyes—yes, her grandmother's eyes were hooded just like the ones in the picture.

Tessa tried to find nice things to say, but cringed immediately after the words left her mouth, because they all sounded like insults. "She looks smart." "She's got a nice smile." During it her eyes kept trying to slide away, to return to the girl on the left. It was strange, but her grandmother almost looked *better* in a way now that she was old, because at least women in their nineties weren't supposed to be beautiful. At least now Grise was allowed to simply exist.

Something that kept Tessa awake that night: looking at the picture, she had been unable to separate Grise's youthful appearance from the way she looked when she was old. There was no way for her to see her grandmother as a young woman, not even when she was staring at a photo of it, not even when this young woman's face was right in front of her eyes.

It seemed that this was part of the loneliness of growing old. The loneliness of reaching a point where no one who was still alive would ever have seen you as a young person. In the end, your true self—because everyone thought of their young self as their true self, as the person at the core of their being—died long before you did. All those people and all those pictures going back and back and back, and with each generation the images growing blurrier and more muted, falling into the vastness of the past.

CHAPTER SEVEN

BLYTHE, CALIFORNIA, 2014

Alistair succeeded in booking a gig at the Shot Glass for the Friday of that week. It only took them a few hours to drive to Blythe, but the journey seemed much longer. The Mojave Desert swallowed up time, and everything else was exaggerated: colors, sounds. The air was not thinner in terms of oxygen, but visually and aurally it was thinner, more translucent. There was a murkiness to the air up North and in colder places that did not exist in the desert. Colors were brighter here, the edges of things sharper, objects sucked into your vision and spat back out at you in hyperreal clarity.

It was a hundred and fifteen degrees. The desert floor shimmered with heat. At one point, the air conditioning broke and, before they figured out how to fix it, they endured half an hour of near-panic, drinking water as fast as it seeped back out of their skin. The sky glared down on them, brilliant merciless blue, an eye without sclera or pupil. To a bystander, Tessa thought, the RV might resemble a dusty, banged-up beetle crawling across the desert.

"It'll be worth it," Alistair told her. They were in the back of the RV; Zac was driving. He spoke to her quietly, as though this were something intimate they were sharing, not something he had told the other members of the band as well.

The Shot Glass was in the center of town. It looked like nothing during the day, just another building, but at night it was a lit-up box. It was mostly windows, and the lights inside turned it into a red-orange cube, like the light of a womb illuminated by a flashlight. There were even threads of darker red in the windows like veins, which upon closer inspection turned out to be thin, curved railings. It was at odds with the architecture of the rest of the town, which leaned quaint, western (and seemed to be mostly empty). The Shot Glass was like someone had taken a club from New York City and plopped it down on the opposite coast.

They got to the venue around 6 p.m. on the day they were set to perform, to set up the gear and do sound checks. Inside it was pure and hollow. It reminded Tessa of those glass houses in architectural magazines, or the kind that always got robbed in movies: rich people walking around an immense open space, holding glasses of sloshing red wine, throwing their heads back in brittle laughter. Except this wasn't a house but a performance space. There were no rooms, just the floor and the backstage and the bar. The ceiling stretched up perhaps fifty feet, with three stories' worth of balconies and staircases ringing the walls, skinny banisters and thin floors that looked like they might not support the weight of a full audience.

Tessa had some problems setting up the amp, and when Emrys asked her, "Don't you know how to do that by now?" he said it jokingly, but she looked at him, held his gaze until he looked away. She wondered if maybe he guessed that she had overheard him the other day. The feeling didn't scare her but rather excited her. The sense of edging close to some boundary she was not supposed to touch, an electrical field that shimmered with danger.

Today they were performing songs off their latest album, Maiden of Doom. Tessa paced back and forth in the space behind the stage. People began to file in. Tessa couldn't see them but she could hear them, the murmur of voices like a slowly welling sea. The lighting was turned down low, and she peeked her head out to see what they looked like. Oh God. There were so many of them. She felt like she was rocking on waves, back and forth, back and forth. She wished she hadn't had quite so much caffeine this morning.

"This is the biggest show we're playing in months," Alistair said, clearing his throat. They were in the middle of warming up their vocals, and he took a break from the sounds to sip from a glass of water.

"The Shot Glass, more like the Snot Glass," Nico said, adjusting a dial on his bass. "Or the Snob Glass. Did you catch the look on the hostess's face when I introduced myself to her? She looked like she thought I was one of the freakin' junkies off the street."

"That's cause you look like one," Zac said. "It's all the piercings. Also, maybe you should comb your hair."

"You look like you just walked in from Caltech," Nico snapped.

Normally Tessa would jump in, but now she tried not to listen to their bickering, instead thinking ahead to the show. She had heard live performances be compared to many things—sex, drugs, spiritual experiences—but the thing came the closest to her was one drug in particular. She had done Molly three times, spacing it out every few months, and the feeling was almost identical to what she felt when performing: endless energy pulsing from the center of her body, euphoria sizzling through her limbs in a shower of violet-colored sparks. A sense of connection with everyone around her, an invisible cord looped through their chests and around and around the room, a string of lights. The feeling of endurance, her muscles smooth and strong and sleek, like she could go forever.

The thought came to her of performing while *on* Molly. Now, that was something. That would probably make her explode. Pieces of her raining down from the ceiling. *Rain of Flesh,* she thought. It was ridiculously gross; maybe Emrys would appreciate it as a potential song title.

Then, for the thousandth time, she remembered what he had said about her. *We should've cut her after all. I told you guys.* He'd used the tone of voice one might use when saying, *I told you guys we should have put that extra-strong roach poison down.* That same long-suffering, exasperated tone.

They walked out onto the stage. The lights in the space had been turned down, but Tessa was sure that from the outside the room would still look illuminated, if only barely: a ruby-colored jewel, a mute glow.

Why do you care what it looks like from the outside? she thought. *You're here now.* But for a strange, disconnected moment she wished she were one of the people outside, people who had no connection to any of this or even the knowledge that they existed.

The size of the crowd was enormous. Alistair was right: it had been ages since Pestilential Harbor had performed for an audience of this size. There were all sorts of people, and although the positioning of the lights made it hard to pick out details, she caught glimpses of them like flashes of light on water: metal band T-shirts (disappointingly, no Pestilential Harbor T-shirts, although they hadn't marketed those very hard anyway), hoops jammed through nostrils, full sleeve tattoos, stiff leather; there were even a few preppy girls who looked like they might have wandered in from a nearby nightclub.

Maybe the presence of so many people was a good omen. Maybe it was a sign that something was about to change. But when Tessa tried to gather this hope in her mind, tried to let it wash through her, it felt hazy and remote. It felt, bizarrely, like she was trying to get excited about something that was already in the distant past.

Beside her, Alistair was adjusting the height of his mic, and she tried to make eye contact—a wordless *good luck* before they began, perhaps, a *good luck* shared only between the two of them—but he was looking into the audience as if searching for someone. Tessa followed his gaze, scanning for a female face looking back at Alistair, but it was impossible to see who he was looking at; there were so many people, so many faces in the crowd. She was being paranoid. She shook her head, a tiny movement that no one else would see, and mentally ran through the lyrics of the first song. More lights turned on along the sides of the railings, illuminating the edges of the room. The crowd grew quiet in anticipation. The box filled with light.

A sensation that had always followed her throughout every performance: that, while singing, she left her body. The life pouring out of her skin and flesh, out through her mouth and into the words themselves, inhabiting the exhalations in the air. The heavy powerful vocals she pushed out from her stomach, the high notes that made her throat feel like a crystal chamber: something of her spiraling out of her body and leaving her until the end of the show, upon which it would return to her, a phantom slipping back into its shell.

Tonight she did not feel this.

Their first song of the night was loosely based on the story of a siren who lured sailors to their deaths, but fell in love with one of the men she sang to. By the time she realized what was going to happen to him, it was too late. She watched him dive into the water and tried to save him, but was unable to do so, and so had no choice but to watch him drown. From that day on, she sang only to his corpse, visiting it where it rotted deep beneath the surface, full of despair and regret over how she had murdered her love.

When Emrys had told them the story last month—it was he who wrote most of the lyrics, or at least the stories around them—Alistair asked, "She really didn't realize what was going to happen to him? Hadn't she been doing this for years now? A bit slow, wasn't she?"

"Yeah, we're gonna have a song about a brain-dead mermaid now?" Nico tugged at an earring, huffing a laugh.

Emrys looked around the RV, his small mouth tight. "Sirens are different from humans, you know. They live for thousands of years. They process time on a different scale."

"Dude, they're not *real*," Zac said. Everyone besides Emrys was laughing by now; Tessa fell into Alistair's shoulder in hysterics. "You do *know* that, right?"

"And why couldn't she save him?" Alistair persisted. His arm came up around Tessa for a moment, not enough for anyone else to notice, but she felt it, and a frisson of excitement coursed up her spine. "Couldn't she just kind of hold his head above the water until one of his mates came to save him? Doggy-paddling, or whatever the mermaid equivalent is?"

"Jesus, it's a story. I'm not Hemingway, I'm just trying to write some lyrics. I thought this was a cool, tragic story. Clearly I was wrong."

This incident, along with many others, was proof that the other members of the band didn't see Emrys as their leader, and in fact even made fun of him much of the time—certainly more than they made fun of Zac or Tessa or Alistair. Maybe Emrys had felt that if he turned their hostilities to another member, one who was easy to single out based on gender, he would become more respected. But it wasn't like they didn't respect him. And, *and*, if he felt disrespected, why couldn't he just say so, instead of conspiring against her? Or maybe he truly did feel she was dead weight and this had nothing to do with him feeling disrespected.

These thoughts came to Tessa in pieces, between songs. By their third song she was still thinking about Siren's Lament, her mind stuck on those lyrics and the story behind them, and almost messed up her words. Her voice stuttered as she recovered her part in the song, and when she got back on track she was half a beat behind. She had to skip a word to catch up. No one in the audience seemed to notice, but Alistair glanced at her, frowning, dark eyebrows drawing together above his jutting nose.

Sorry, she mouthed when her part was over, but he was singing by now, his eyelids fluttering closed, and he did not see her.

After the show, Tessa went backstage and noticed that Alistair was gone. When she asked the other members of the band, trying to seem casual about it, none of them had even seen him leave.

"Man, even I usually wait till after we pack up," Nico whined. "Do you think he saw some really hot chick and couldn't wait anymore?"

Zac shrugged. "Maybe. He could've given us the courtesy of hanging around a few more minutes, though."

Tessa concentrated on putting the equipment away. Her hands felt cold. It was the reverse of how she usually felt: during the performance she had remained entirely within herself, but now she had gone away and was not coming back, some essential part of herself still out there in the space where the audience had assembled, guttering like a candle flame.

She remembered Alistair looking into the audience, that searching gaze as he scanned the crowd. Had he been looking for someone in particular, or was it her imagination?

Ten minutes later, he came back. He seemed breathless as he jogged backstage, asking, "What'd I miss?"

"Nothing, dude," Zac said. "What did *we* miss?"

"Not much. Just had a conversation with the manager. Thanked him for letting us play."

The others seemed satisfied with this explanation, but Tessa found herself scanning his appearance, searching for lipstick marks on his shirt or an undone fly. *This is why you don't get involved with bandmates.*

They went outside the RV to smoke and drink and talk about anything other than music for a few hours. Eventually Emrys went in, and then Alistair left and went off to the other side of the RV. She felt like this might be her cue to follow. She walked after him, her footsteps soft in the grass.

He turned when he heard her, but he looked surprised. "Hey," he said. There was a bunched energy in his body, something coiled and potent, a tension waiting to be released.

"Hey." She took an inhale from her joint and breathed out a long snake of smoke, watching it disperse in the air. "Want to tell me where you were after the show?"

She knew immediately it had been the wrong thing to ask. And she'd asked it in the worst possible way, like a bitchy, nagging wife. Her insides cringed against themselves: she was turning into Holly.

Alistair's features folded inwards as his face contracted to a point, narrow and guarded. "I certainly don't now."

If there were a way to take back the last few seconds, to haul them backwards like scooping clay, she would. But this was impossible. She thought wildly: *The past is unchangeable.* The words flew into and then out of her head, a murmur of birds.

"I just meant I'm curious," she attempted. It sounded lame to her, and evidently to him too, because he just looked out at the night. She followed his gaze, trying to think of something, anything else. Alistair hadn't been gone long enough to fuck someone, and it didn't really matter if he had anyway, or if he'd been flirting or getting a girl's number. She and Alistair weren't dating. She had no claim to him.

From here, half of the city was laid out before them. The ground was speckled with lights, like a sky peppered with stars. It looked cozy and peaceful, but it also did not look like a place that would be friendly to a doom metal band.

When she shared this thought with him he said, "Yeah, it's amazing the turnout we had tonight. But that's something I love about California. It's not like Minnesota, where I grew up. There are all kinds of people here."

This was all wrong. He was talking to her like she was an acquaintance. His tone was friendly and removed and not the least bit intimate. She began to sweat. She had been sweating onstage, too, and now the residual heat crept back into her skin, spreading out underneath it. She was terribly aware of herself all of a sudden, of the physicality of her body: striated muscles shrouded in yellow clumps of fat, all of it wrapped around a skeleton. She thought of the drowned sailor again. Wondered if he even realized for a second, as he was dying, that the siren who had sung him to his doom was trying to save him. If it mattered to him at all. If it wasn't actually pretty fucking self-indulgent of that siren to sing to him, day after day, to his unhearing and unfeeling corpse.

"I'm glad we did it," she said. "The show, I mean. I think it's going to be really good for us. Someone's bound to sit up and take notice."

Now he seemed responsive. He smiled. "I think so, too. We should be on an upswing after this. Could you not blow that right in my face, please?"

"Sorry."

"Thanks."

She wanted to scream.

Above them the moon glowed as if lit from within. She couldn't always see the face of the man in the full moon, but tonight she could. He had a round mouth, a gaping and helpless expression. It was like looking into the face of a child being tortured—or rather, an adult who was being tortured but who had something wrong with them mentally, so they didn't even know what was happening, or why. Her stomach felt brittle and porous and cold. She looked away.

CHAPTER EIGHT

SAN DIEGO, CALIFORNIA, 2024

Shortly after she returned from New York, Tessa's most recent impression of her grandmother—the way she had appeared on the visit, her confusion and her fear—faded slightly. As always, she looked up Methuselah, even though there had been no fires lately. She let her gaze spiral across its outstretched arms, its corkscrew branches. *My old friend,* she thought. *My very old friend.* It had seen generations of her ancestors live and die. In comparison to it, Tessa was nothing more than a speck, a momentary blot of light.

She opened a new page and clicked from one news article to the next, her unease growing as she moved from story to story. China's economy was steadily on track to overtake that of the US—although, the article added, their average standard of living was still well below that of Americans, because they simply had so many people. Was that supposed to make her feel better, thinking of other peoples' suffering? She clicked through the photos at the end of the article: millions of stacked cage houses. Boxes like vertical prisons extending from the earth.

On the next page: Neuralink, the brainchild (ha) of tech billionaire Elon Musk, had recently begun its human trial phase. The article promised that with this brain-computer interface, no thought would ever have to be lost, no idea would ever disappear into the ether. The article assumed that its reader was just as excited about this prospect as Musk himself was.

Tessa remembered the days when there had been talk of Neuralink promising new treatments for paralysis, of enabling those who were disabled to live fulfilling lives. Now those ideas seemed to have fallen by the wayside. Now, it seemed, being a regular biological human was a disability in and of itself. *No thought will ever be lost!* the article crowed, as though thoughts were supposed to be kept around forever, as though they were not formless, shapeless, invisible for a reason. Every motion, every human transaction, was already recorded: Tessa could not walk down the streets of San Diego or New York or Texas without her movements being tracked and filed away forever. She had an app on her phone that tracked her steps, her metabolism, her blood pressure. Her heartbeat. You could turn it off, but most people never bothered to. Soon every thought, too, would be recorded.

She buried her head in her hands. Her palms fit the curve of her skull exactly, the heels of her hands pressing into her eye sockets. She imagined humans cradling their skulls and comforting themselves in this way since the beginning of time. Then she imagined a neural link inside her brain, a mechanism that would enable her to connect directly to a computer. A feeling of horror suffused her, a horror so intense that it made her head swim. Dizzying tilt, vertigo, a piece of her spinning off into blackness.

She remembered her grandmother saying she wanted to go home, and Tessa thought that now she understood.

When she lifted her head again the room seemed smaller. At the sight of the walls—so narrow, almost as though they were closing in—her biceps twitched involuntarily. Blood pulsed in her ears. She wanted to run, or fight, or punch something. But all she could do was grind her teeth and stare at her hands: at the knuckles, the wrinkles, the veins, everything that marked her as human. Hideously, beautifully human.

I have to get out, she thought, her mind a frantic whirl. *I have to leave.*

But go where? Where?

And the answer came to her in a flash, as though the blood pulsating through her head had taken on its own intelligence and was speaking directly to her from inside her own skull: *To Methuselah.*

She couldn't, of course. She had no idea where the tree was. But she could do something close: she could get out of the city, away from civilization itself. Because despite what the news articles seemed to want her to believe, there were still places that had not been burned to gray ash or paved and fitted with centers for implanting Neuralink chips. Out there, somewhere, there was still dirt, grass, green.

There were still trees.

She opened a new window in her browser and began searching for wilderness retreats. Then she went back and closed all the other windows, because her computer was beginning to overheat. Continued searching. There were so many of these places, but none of them seemed to offer what she was looking for. There were wine and yoga retreats, horseback-riding retreats, couples' retreats. She clicked from one list to the next until a cramp began to develop in her forearm, and she had to roll her wrists back and forth. *Not getting any younger,* she thought, and then she remembered Methuselah and stifled a laugh. Oh, but she was *young.*

Then, on the next page, she saw it. The Lodge: a Northern California Wilderness retreat. The page had a picture of a woman gazing at a row of sunlit mountains, and it read: *Reconnect to nature. Nestled at the base of the Cascade Mountains, The Lodge is a detox perfect for families, couples, or solo travelers. Relax and recharge in the wilderness. For the two weeks of the program, cell phones are forbidden, as well as Internet access (so you'll have to go elsewhere to upload your photographs). Overall this is a place to relax and enjoy yourself. The remote north and the beauty of the mountains will remind you of the restorative power of nature, and the potential that rests within you.*

She liked the tone of the article writer. It almost seemed like they were poking fun at the people who went to wilderness retreats to take photos for Instagram.

She called her father. "Don't be alarmed when I don't talk to you for a couple weeks," she told him. "I'm going off the grid."

There was silence, and she pictured her father taking the phone away from his ear so he could stare at it. "What do you mean?" he finally said.

"I'm going on a wilderness retreat. It's a kind of technology detox thing—no phones or internet access. Just the mountains."

"What about your work?"

"I can take a couple weeks off. I haven't used my vacation for this year yet." In fact, she had used so little vacation time that her boss had grown concerned. "Enjoy yourself,

Tessa!" she often insisted. "You don't have to work *all* the time."

Her father, still sounding slightly bemused, told her to have fun. After hanging up the phone, Tessa went into the kitchen to see what she could scrounge up for a snack. She missed Pearl's cooking. The produce in stores seemed to be getting worse lately; the peaches she'd bought the other day were turning straight from hard to rotten without passing through a stage of ripeness in between.

She thought of the Cascade Mountains. They wouldn't have any Methuselahs, but they did have a dense conifer forest: red cedars, Douglas firs, hemlocks, spruce trees. The scent of evergreen trees always made her think of winter, and not any California winter, but an imagined winter, a winter the way winter had been two hundred years ago: huge swathes of snow, temperatures that plummeted well below zero. Landscapes blanketed in snow and ice. Winters like these still existed in places on Earth, of course—there was Canada, and Antarctica, and Siberia—but even in Siberia there had been temperatures over a hundred degrees lately. And wildfires. Wildfires in Siberia—it sounded like a paradox, a riddle.

She abandoned the peaches and went back to the computer. Staring at the screen, she thought: What if there was nowhere to escape to? This retreat promised an escape, but you were still crawling over the same globe like a doomed insect; you could not get off of it, could not fly away somewhere else. You were chained to its surface.

But then Tessa imagined closing the browser window and not trying, returning to her life, not taking her vacation. Perhaps signing up herself for the next phase of Neuralink trials.

Her hand twitched towards the payment button.

Another window opened when she clicked on it. The cost was two thousand dollars. For a moment the figure made her hesitate, but then: she had thousands saved. She wasn't trying to save it for anything in particular; she simply could not imagine what she might spend it on. It was piling up like dust in an empty house.

By the time she closed her laptop and went to bed, she had purchased her space in the program. She had the receipt on her phone, and in her email, and saved as a screenshot for good measure. She had also purchased a plane ticket. The next session started in two weeks' time. She went to sleep dreaming of Northern California, and what she might find there.

On the first day of April, the rain started as if it had been released from behind a dam. The air was tight with moisture. Over the next few days the scent of healthy flowers turned into something rotten and dank, too much water clogging everything up. Soil running loose and liquid, mold softening and dripping.

It's completely strange, Tessa's coworker Charlie typed. *I thought we were supposed to be in the middle of all these droughts.*

Another message: *I haven't spoken to a real live human being in days. I feel like I'm going a little wacko, lol.*

Come with me, Tessa suggested impulsively. *I'm going to a wilderness retreat in a few days, but there's probably still time for you to sign up.*

Blinking cursor, three dots appearing, then disappearing, then reappearing again. Finally, Charlie wrote: *Can't afford the time off. But you have fun!!*

Are you sure?

Absolutely. But you have fun!!!!

Tessa let the conversation end there, because the number of exclamation points Charlie was using only seemed to be growing.

The day before she left for the retreat, her father called her with the news that her grandmother was in the hospital. "What happened?" Tessa asked.

"Nothing really happened...as such. She's just...old. Very old."

She could hear the exhaustion in his voice, and prepared to offer to stay. He must have guessed what she was going to say, because he said, "Don't you dare. I called you because I thought you should know, but I don't want you to cancel your trip on my account. When are you supposed to leave, by the way?"

"Tomorrow."

"Oh, no. I shouldn't have called you, Tessa. I'm sorry."

"It's okay. At least this way I know."

That night, she woke up three times. She thought she might be able to sleep on the airplane, but this was a pipe dream; as it turned out, the ride was loud and irritating, the dips of the plane giving her a queasy feeling every few minutes. She mostly kept her head down until she was able to escape the airport, and before getting a car to the retreat, she stood outside to breathe in the air for a few minutes.

Up here, seven hundred miles north of San Diego, it was noticeably cooler. The wind that came in from the mountains smelled like honey. The heavy rain had ceased, fading to a light drizzle and then simply to a fine mist that hung in the air. She checked and re-checked the destination before tapping the address into her ride sharing app. A car pulled up next to the airport a few minutes later.

The retreat was nestled at the foot of Mount Shasta. Around it: towering, ancient volcanoes, covered in smooth glaciers; rivers cutting like cold blue veins through the heart of the landscape. She didn't absorb it until she stepped out of the car. Then the world opened around her, origami unfolding and revealing every leaf and tree and shard of stone that had been hiding along its creases.

Before her extended three long wooden two-story houses, interconnected and sprawling outwards from a central point. There were many-faceted glass windows in their sides, and low sliding glass doors in the front. The walls were the shade of birch bark, pale and unsaturated, as if to throw the colors of the surrounding area into even greater intensity.

A woman was coming down the path to greet her. Something in Tessa, some knot of tension she hadn't even known was there, relaxed upon seeing that it was a woman. She had long brown hair with glints of red in it, and when she smiled, Tessa saw that she actually had wrinkles around her mouth and between her forehead, rather than the stretched, taut skin that was so common among people in their forties and fifties. "Welcome to The Lodge," she said. "My name is Natasha."

"Tessa Tanner." She expected the woman to look her name up on her phone, but Natasha just nodded in recognition, as though she had already memorized the names of every guest. "I guess this is when I surrender my phone?"

Natasha laughed. "I guess it is. Any last-minute email checking?"

Tessa glanced at the screen one last time—although she had been looking at it constantly in the car—and saw something that caused her stomach to drop. It was a message from her father. *Grandma awake now. Thought you'd want to know. Love, Dad.*

She stared at the text for long seconds. Her father never put the word "love" in his messages, preferring instead to act as though they were good friends. He seemed to disregard the strict boundaries of parenthood; like Holly, he saw no reason they couldn't be pals as well as father and child.

She kept reading and re-reading the words. Maybe her father was so stressed he'd texted her without thinking, without recalling where she was. Or perhaps he had intended the text as good news, as something to perk her up before her retreat from civilization. Good news, though? What could be good about a ninety-four year old woman waking up in a hospital bed, away from the only home she'd known for the last half-century?

"Okay, done," she said, and passed her phone to Natasha.

"No second thoughts?"

"Nope. I'm all set." She followed Natasha into the lodge. The interior of the building smelled like wood and fire-smoke and sawdust. There was more of that honey scent, too, a wild sweetness.

The text was spreading inside her, the information contained within it moving outwards to the edges of her like pooling water. She was in the middle of the wilderness, yet she couldn't shake the mental image of her grandmother lying in a hospital, drenched in its relentless artificial daylight, crying out that she wanted to go home. She reminded herself that it wasn't *that* bad, that the old woman wasn't completely alone in the world—she had her son, of course, and Holly had been calling her every week—but the image persisted.

Natasha introduced her to a group of people, explaining

that she was the last to arrive. Tessa said hello to each of them and promptly forgot their names. There were far fewer other people than she'd expected: only nine, including Natasha.

Natasha gave an introductory speech, describing the region they were located in, the topography that surrounded them and its history. "In the early parts of the nineteenth century, before the colonization of the West, there were many people who lived within view of this mountain. None of them are tribes you have probably heard of. The Modoc, the Okwanuchu, the Karuk, the Yana—the Shasta, of course —yep, just what I thought, blank faces. So much of history disappears without a trace. It makes you wonder what will be left even of us, although we are so certain we're going to preserve every minute detail for eternity. Maybe those tribes were certain of it as well. And now nobody remembers them."

Tessa wondered if Natasha had read about the Neuralink trials too.

"But! I'm getting too sad right now." She began talking about the amenities available there, the hiking and boating and climbing they would do. As Tessa listened, she realized her excitement was already winding down. She wasn't even sure why she had come here. *Reconnect to nature,* the retreat's website had said. But how could you reconnect to something you were never even connected to in the first place? After all, gazing obsessively at a picture on a screen didn't count as connection. Just like what she'd had with Alistair, or with Jupiter, had not been connection either.

Upstairs, her room was breezy and cool, overlooking a cluster of evergreens. She could just glimpse the edge of a river in the distance, the sun glinting on its constantly moving surface. Water shimmering like distant jewels. She unpacked her clothes, pills, toiletries, and notebook. She wasn't sure why she'd brought a notebook; she couldn't remember the last time she had written anything more than a scribbled note longhand.

The lodge contained not just a dining room and bedrooms but a games room and a library. The books in it, Natasha explained, had been gathered from yard sales and library giveaways and novels abandoned at the ends of people's driveways. It was a collection of orphaned volumes, some of them seemingly brand new, some water-damaged and dog-eared and older than Tessa.

Since it was the first day, it was a low-key one. Everyone gathered together for dinner in the lodge dining hall, which took up both stories, the ceiling stretching high overhead. There were farm-fresh eggs, chicken, vegetables, everything organic and sustainably raised. The food was delicious. It tasted sharper and clearer than the meals Tessa was used to eating. She wasn't sure if this was a quality of the food itself, or of her own mindset—that she was somehow enhancing the flavors of what she was eating by paying more attention to them, instead of using one hand to hold her phone in front of her face and the other to shovel pasta into her mouth.

She began talking to the older woman, whose name she had forgotten. She eventually found out that it was Violet, thanks to someone else saying her name from across the table. Violet spoke in an accent Tessa could not place— Peruvian, maybe, or Iranian. Her eyes were a dusty, greenish gray. She, too, had a lined face, although she was probably about twenty years older than Natasha.

"I'm overwhelmed by Natasha's welcome," she said. "And the beauty of the landscape is..." She searched for the right word, and finally just smiled. "Beautiful."

Tessa found herself thinking, none too charitably, that Violet was a recently divorced woman, or perhaps a grandmother whose children had long since left the nest, searching for fulfillment outside of the family. She agreed with Violet about the beauty of their surroundings, but the more she talked about them, the less certain she felt. As though her opinions, when shared with another person, became less real and less true.

She mentioned Neuralink at one point, without meaning to. A man across the table said it was like something out of a sci-fi horror movie. The woman next to him said that he had the sci-fi part right, but definitely *not* the horror part, and they began to argue quietly.

Violet watched them with a look of amusement. "See what you started?" she said to Tessa in a light, teasing tone. Tessa wasn't sure how she felt about this. They didn't seem to be close enough for teasing.

"It's okay," Violet continued. "People are always going to have reactions to things. But I don't pay attention to... things like what you mentioned. The whole idea of that invention seems terrible to you, no? So why talk about it? That's why I don't pay attention."

"You don't pay attention to anything happening now?"

She immediately wished she could take back her words, but Violet didn't seem offended. "Those things aren't important as you may think. I cannot tell you what to do, of course, but I'm just enjoying my time here. That is the point. To be away from it all, not...not connected to everything like a hive of bees. It makes me feel like my head is buzzing."

"I've felt like that too," Tessa said. "I do agree. It's not a great feeling. But how is it not important, what's happening around us?"

Violet smiled. "I have only been here a day, but I do know that in the soon future, no one is going to come marching up to this lodge and implant any kind of link into my head. And as long as that is true, I'm not going to let myself worry about it. What I am certain about is that one day—in the soon future—I won't be here anymore. I'll be a part of these plants and these rocks and this soil, all around us. That is what I prefer to think of the future as."

It took Tessa a moment to realize that she wasn't being poetic, but actually talking about being dead. A shiver moved over her skin. Tessa didn't find her words comforting, but she didn't find them completely terrifying, either. Maybe it was Violet's calm tone as she spoke. Or maybe it was the way she appeared to be exactly the age she was, neither unhealthy and prematurely aged nor desperately clinging onto youth.

Tessa continued eating her meal. As she did so, she became conscious of how it was temporary, how eventually her and it and everyone around her would be nothing but rot and soil. The idea quickly became overwhelming and she tried not to think about it. Maybe when she was Violet's age she would be more accepting of everything. Right now she preferred to take it one day, one second at a time.

That night she had a dream that the lodge was gone and she was waking up in a grim steel-lined room. "Congratulations," said the man standing over her. He was removing something from her head, and she felt a coolness on her scalp. When she put her hand to her head, she felt nothing but short bristles, like those of a toothbrush: all of her hair had been shaved off. "You have successfully completed the first trial of Neuralink 5.0's wilderness-immersion experience." His pupils flexed at her, geometric and angular, as he spoke.

She looked dumbly up at him. "Huh?"

He explained patiently: "You were part of our very first round of human trials. Neuralink 5.0 has made it possible to experience long-gone things such as forests, wooden buildings, and sustained, long-term human interactions."

Tessa woke up, mouth sour, chest slick with sweat.

CHAPTER NINE

BLYTHE, CALIFORNIA, 2014

Three days after the gig at the Shot Glass, Pestilential Harbor was still celebrating their newest success. Nico actually cashed out for a restaurant, Japanese of all things, and they sauntered in—Nico first, with his piercings and wild hair, aesthetically more the face of the band than anyone else—and then Emrys and Zac, and finally Tessa and Alistair.

The previous day, Alistair had been gone for hours. They all went off and did their own thing during the day when they weren't recording, but Tessa had noticed him leaving during the afternoon without an explanation—something noticeable in itself, as they always told the others if they were going somewhere—and coming back when it was nearly evening. She'd spent the rest of the night in a knot of anxiety, staring up sleeplessly through the RV's roof window.

But maybe whatever it had been hadn't gone so well. Because she thought she noticed Alistair walking closer to her than he'd been doing the day of the performance, looking at her more. She wondered when they would be able to stay in a motel again, when it would be just the two of them in their own room. It had been nearly a week, and she kept reminding herself not to get too attached to the idea, but her body wouldn't listen; every time she caught sight of the curve of his nose, she would remember how it had felt nestled between her legs. How his tongue, his hands, other parts of him had felt there. Her knees were watery as she sat down beside him, her breath thin and hot in her chest.

The restaurant was like the reverse of the Shot Glass: small windows, dark tablecloths, wood-paneled walls. They ordered drinks, and then Alistair looked around the table, cleared his throat. His hands were tapping on his lap, something only Tessa could see.

Alistair said, "I've been wanting to tell you guys something. I put it off for a while, but this is as good a time as any."

Tessa thought, sharp as a reflex: *He's sick.*

"An A&R Rep came to the show the other day, and he wants to represent me. I've signed with him. I asked about all of you, but he thinks I'll do better on my own. I'm sorry you had to find out this way, but honestly—I couldn't find another way to tell you."

Nobody said anything. Tessa wanted to ask him how this had happened so suddenly, but the words snarled together like tangling limbs, collapsed back down into her stomach. She thought: *This is where he was the other day. This was who he was looking for in the crowd. He planned this whole thing before even booking the show.*

Alistair swallowed and kept talking. "It's a fairly big label, but there's no guarantee of success. The A&R Rep, though, that guy, he really did like me. He was the one I was talking to the other day after the show. And yesterday, too.

He helped me set up the show in the first place, and he obviously liked my performance, and he liked the rest of you guys too, of course, but not enough to sign you. But I wasn't going to turn him down, was I? I mean, would you, if you were the one he'd approached?"

Even as Tessa felt that the ground was canting underneath her, she thought: *Stop talking, you idiot! You're just making everything worse!* And another part of her was disappointed in him for babbling so much, for making so many excuses.

Nico began laughing. Emrys' face had drained of color, and Zac was squinting from Tessa to Alistair as though she might have had something to do with it, but Nico just laughed and laughed and laughed. "You sneaky fucker," he said through his chortles. "Very funny. What a hoot! You owe me shumai for that."

Alistair grew a shade paler, but his jaw set and he said, "Nico. I'm not kidding. This isn't a joke."

Nico's laughs died, one by one, like bubbles popping in the air. When he spoke again, his voice was flat. "You're serious."

"Bro, he's for real," Zac said in a low voice.

Nico's nostrils flared. "You little fuck. This is why you picked a restaurant to tell us, so we'd be in public. So we wouldn't make a scene."

"I didn't—"

"Well, I'M GONNA MAKE A SCENE," Nico roared, and stood up, thrusting his hands under the table and jerking it upwards. Tessa yelped. But it was too heavy for him to flip, and he only managed to jostle it enough to send their drinks sloshing. Yelling in pain, he jerked his hands away. They dangled loosely; it looked like he had sprained both wrists.

Utter silence. Everyone in the restaurant was looking at them. A busboy several tables away had paused with his hand frozen in the process of picking up a plate. Tessa could practically hear the sweat trickling down Alistair's face.

Nico stood there motionless for a few moments, a glitching film still, before storming out. They listened to his footsteps as he left the restaurant, the *whoosh* of the door—he couldn't slam it, it wasn't that type of door—as he shouldered it closed as hard as he could behind him.

"Congratulations," Zac managed. It sounded like he was forcing the words out. "So what kind of label is this? How big are we talking? Big, right?"

"Are you going to scream at me too," Alistair said in a monotone. He wasn't looking in anyone's eyes; his gaze was fixed on the tablecloth. The black expanse looked to Tessa like a starless sky, a mute sea.

"So you basically auditioned for them during the show."

"Not at the show. He wanted to see me during the show, and yes, it's true, I auditioned yesterday—"

"But you didn't bring us to the audition. We didn't get to audition...*with* you. The audition was *just* for you."

"Zac, come on. He didn't want all of us. I couldn't insist on you guys coming. He's a busy guy."

"Well, thanks for trying," Emrys said sarcastically. His features looked too large for his face, as though his skull had shrunk. "At least you put in some effort, right? Or no? Did you just leap at the chance to leave us hanging?"

"You're not hanging! You still have Tessa."

"Hey, wait a minute." Tessa couldn't look directly at Alistair, either; she could only look at the edges of his face, just beyond his gaze. But not for the same reason she used to be unable to look at him during videos of their performances. No, this was for a different reason entirely. "Are you trying to make them feel worse?"

Emrys's expression of confusion was not convincing.

"Since I'm dead weight," she continued. Zac frowned, but Emrys' face grew blank with shock. "That's what you said, right? And Alistair had to convince you I wasn't."

"So now he's your hero," Zac said. "Great. Are you going to join his new band, too? You gonna sign with him? Oh, wait, doesn't look like it from what he just said, does it? So why are you siding with him?"

She ignored Zac. "Why aren't you talking?" she demanded of Emrys, whose face was still blank. "You were the one who suggested it in the first place, that you kick me out."

"Do we have to do this here?" Emrys said. His tone was blank too, empty as though with boredom, and this enraged Tessa further. Nico had left, but his furious energy remained, filling the crevices between Tessa's fingers, seeping into her pores. The more bored Emrys looked, the angrier she got. She could feel her own heartbeat, the muscle juddering frantically behind her ribs. "Why not? What better place is there? At least we're giving them a show, right?"

Emrys just looked at her.

"Since you said I was dead weight." But she had said this already, and it sounded lame the second time, like she was trying to drive a point home that had not had the impact she'd hoped. Her words had no force behind them.

"Yeah, you did," Alistair said, as though suddenly remembering that he was supposed to be on her side.

Emrys just shook his head, like, *Okay, so?*

Tessa snorted in disgust and tried to get up, but the table was too close to the wall, so she had to scoot out on her ass, her pants making squeaking sounds against the vinyl. The stares of the restaurant patrons had begun to feel less like those of an audience and more like those of a circle of onlookers around the village freak.

Outside the restaurant, the setting sun was a burning knot in the sky. The clouds sweeping after it looked miles long. A cool wind was gusting into the air, fanning it out in a breeze, breaking up the heat and scattering it in invisible particles across the desert.

Alistair had followed her out of the restaurant. Onstage he had been a force, majestic and tragic and noble, a drowning sailor pulled to the depths by the woman he loved; now he looked smaller.

"He's a coward," she told him. "And so are you, by the way. Thanks for letting us believe we were, as you put it, on the upswing, only to surprise us with this wonderful news."

He caught up with her, and she began walking again. Beyond them, just past the outer reaches of town, was the open breadth of the desert, and beyond it, the mountains. Maybe she could just keep walking, out into the desert, just keep walking and walking. The mountains would stay the same distance away from her no matter how far she went, even if she walked until she collapsed.

"Where are you going?" he asked.

She wanted to say *Into the desert*, but this would be too dramatic and wasn't even true. She wasn't going to walk into the desert. This wasn't a movie. She was going to walk until her feet started hurting, or until she got hungry—they never had gotten their shumai—and then go back to the RV and accept whatever was happening in her life.

"Why did you lie to me?" she asked. "Why did you tell me—in the RV, when we were going across the Mojave—

that the performance would be good for us? You meant it would be good for *you*. So why didn't you just say so?"

"You think I should've told you guys before the performance? How do you think it would've gone then?"

"I guess it wouldn't have turned out too good," she said. "For you." She found a rock, sat down on it. It was a big rock, but the fact remained—she was sitting on a rock, covered in dust swept in from the desert. She kept thinking about the desert, the terrible burning expanse of it.

He sat down next to her. He was still doing that thing with his hands, tapping his fingers against his thighs. He probably wasn't even aware he was doing it. The movement was frantic, the jerking motions of a trapped animal. Every other part of him was perfectly still.

"I'm not jealous of you." She laughed. "Or, okay, I am. But I'm not, like, angry at you for that. I'm angry at you for lying to me and making me think I had a future—well, making all of us think we had a future, but I'm not going to fight those guys' battles for them after what they said about me—making me think I had a future when I didn't. And don't say I'm being dramatic," she added, seeing him open his mouth. "I mean a future in the terms *you* spoke about it: a future as a band, as Pestilential Harbor, the five of us, starting the other night. That was not true."

"I know. I'm sorry. I'm really sorry, Tessa."

Long silence. Nobody else had come out from the restaurant; maybe Zac and Emrys had ended up ordering food after all. The shadows on the ground stretched out, growing taller and thinner, angling sideways across the dirt. Throwing darkness.

"How did you meet this A&R Rep anyway?" she asked eventually.

"I got in contact with him online. I thought maybe he

could represent all of us—honestly. I sent him a link to our music and it turned out he was into it. He asked me if we were coming to any shows in the area, and I told him no, and he said he could help me schedule one..." He shrugged. "Back then I still thought he wanted to see all of us, not just me."

There was still something Tessa wasn't getting.

"But what made this guy different? We've reached out to dozens of reps since we started, and nothing has come from any of them."

"This guy...he went to school with my older brother. I didn't know he'd gotten into music until I looked him up the other day."

"So you had a connection with him from the beginning. You in particular, above the rest of us."

"Yeah, but I wasn't trying to get him to only pay attention to me. I was trying to get him to take notice of all of us."

"And yet, somehow, you were the one he wanted to hear audition, the one who got signed. Ha. It really is all about connections in the end."

He laughed a little, and she looked at him, startled. "I don't mean to laugh, sorry. It's just that you sounded so worn-out. Like you're some jaded forty-year-old business-man. You haven't gotten to *the end* of anything, Tessa. There's still plenty of chances for you guys."

"He didn't like me, did he." It was not something that needed to be asked, but she asked it anyway. That need to hear the answer to a question that had been circulating in her brain since Alistair's announcement, even though the answer was already stamped in there.

"It's not that he didn't *like* you—" That placating, condescending tone.

"Whatever. You know what I mean. He didn't want to

hear me audition, either. The couple days after the show, you were the only one he wanted to hear audition." She bit her lip, which swelled, sluglike, under her teeth. "Right?"

"You know you messed up a little during the performance," he said, looking sheepish.

"I messed up *once!* I got—I mixed up the lyrics for, like, one single second, and the rest of it was good, amazing, I was on fire, I was at least as good as you—" She cut off, her throat beginning to tickle with irritation. With those last few words, Alistair had turned his head away from her, looking out across the sprawl of the town. Tessa couldn't even keep arguing in good conscience. She was a good vocalist, but she didn't have the pipes of Tarja or Simone Simons. She was good enough to make people say, "Gee whiz, that's a good singer" when she performed, but not good enough to make them remember her. That was the difference. That was clear by now.

"Could you at least get me an interview?" she asked. It was pathetic, a last-ditch attempt without force or hope behind it.

"I'm sorry, Tessa. But if he'd wanted to hear you, he would have asked for you too, believe me. There was nothing I could do to change his mind about that."

He looked like he was about to say something else, but then didn't.

"What? What were you going to say?"

"I wasn't." And she had to be content with that.

"You'll call me?" she asked.

"I'll call you."

He did not call her. She went back to San Jose, dragging her tail across the San Joaquin Valley, all the way through the sand and the dirt, breathing in dust and coughing up weed smoke like clouds of exhaust. He did not call her.

CHAPTER TEN

NORTHERN CALIFORNIA, 2024

When Tessa opened her eyes again, early in the morning, the nightmare had vanished into the depths of her consciousness. Instead of dread, she felt a lightness buoying her up. She sat up in bed, blinking into the milky pre-dawn. Birds had begun chirping outside the lodge. She tried to identify this new feeling: it was not the lightness of excitement, but something calmer. More serene.

It felt almost like relief. Like a part of her, a part beyond herself, had let go.

When she lay back down and closed her eyes again, an image drifted to the forefront of her mind: her grandmother's face. It was surprisingly easy to picture her, as though they were no longer on the same plane of reality. But the horror Tessa had felt at her appearance the last time she'd seen her was absent. Now that she was no longer thinking of her grandmother as a woman ravaged by time, as someone who had once been a young girl, she could identify a beauty in her. Not the kind of beauty connected to the human form and all the things that were supposedly appealing about it—youth, health, vitality. This was a stranger, older, wilder beauty. The lines on Grise's face like streams branching into tributaries and feeding into the ocean. The puffs of hair clinging to her skull like wisps of cloud. The age spots on her hands like the splotches of pigment on a leaf. The eyes like deep pools of still, untouched water: every part of her returning to nature, just as Grise herself had, finally, sometime just before dawn.

***

After breakfast, the group went on a hike. The three South American travelers bounded ahead, turning their tanned faces up to the sun, shouting with joy. The air smelled raw and crisp. They walked past limestone boulders, through soft beds of grass. The hills around them bloomed with poppies, with bell-like purple flowers and wisps of white, unidentifiable growth like tattered clouds. Evergreens dripped needles sticky and resinous; the dead needles lay fallen around their bases in perfect shadows, circles of light brown paling to orange.

They stopped to eat lunch next to a huge lake, glasslike and smooth, displaying a flipped image of the conifers on all sides. The clouds were thin streaks overhead, white in the sky but muddy in the water. Natasha regaled them with stories about the mythology surrounding the lake, the ancient story of the princess who fell into it and drowned. Tessa pictured what this princess might have looked like: a woman with bronze skin and bone earrings, toes splayed from walking barefoot. She remembered the theory she'd heard years ago from a relative she couldn't place, the theory that all the events of your life were happening simultaneously. Time not a long strip but something folded over and over and over onto itself, every point touching at once. Infinite closeness, infinite detail.

"Have you noticed it's been dry the last few days?" one of the young women was saying to someone else, maybe Leo or Mark.

"Yeah. I'm beginning to think that maybe fire season will start early this year after all."

Tessa looked out over the mountains. For a second, she thought maybe she could see smoke rising from one of the cliffsides, but she peered more closely and the smoke was just a cloud.

"John Muir loved this place," Natasha was saying. "And I quote: 'When I first caught sight of Mount Shasta over the braided folds of the Sacramento Valley, my blood turned to wine, and I have not been weary since.'"

"Are we allowed to drink wine here, though?" someone asked. "Or is that forbidden like cell phones?"

"I'll allow it," said Natasha. "If only because the lodge has a partnership with one of the best wineries in the state."

That night they did have wine: bottles of it under the stars, sitting in a vague circle on the grass outside the lodge. The three travelers, whose names Tessa gradually re-learned as Sam and Christopher and Rio, taught the rest of the group South American songs, and then Margaret told a story about her own experience backpacking through Chile. Tessa mostly listened. She leaned back against the wall of the lodge, absorbing their voices, the shouts in the night: they formed a bracing cage, a vault of sound, keeping the shadows out.

There was nothing particularly special or different about this retreat, she realized; she recalled how she'd hunched over her computer, back in San Diego, clicking through dozens of resorts and comparing them. She had been foolish to agonize so much about which one she picked. The other ones were just like this, only with horse-back-riding or rock climbing or wine tasting mixed in (this didn't count as tasting, it was simply wine imbibing). All that mattered in the end was how Tessa interpreted it.

The constellations glittered far above the ceiling of voices, remote and crystalline. She lowered her gaze to the ground, to the earth. The grass under her thighs was springy, moist with health. She ran her hands over it and wondered when fire season would truly come, when it would spread, when all of this would be scorched. Whether the living grass would still exist in some way, even after it was burned. According to that theory, it would. The living grass existing at the same time as its dead ruins.

She tried to remember who had told her the theory. Her mother? Her father? Her grandmother, when Tessa had been very young?

Violet, sitting next to her, turned and asked, "You are okay?" She spoke over the rim of her wineglass, which was still nearly full. The dark liquid in it formed a smooth mirror, reflecting the stars.

"Yeah, I'm good." Maybe she looked strange, running her fingers through the grass like it was hair.

Violet grinned. "I was like this too, the first time I came out to the country. I was putting my hands on the earth and like...like trying to absorb it inside of me." In her accent, the word *like* was sweet and lilting, her voice turning it into a lyrical sea.

Tessa glanced down at her hands self-consciously. Was that what she'd been doing?

"It's working?" Violet prompted.

"I don't know. I don't think so. I still feel mostly the same. And yesterday I was craving my phone something terrible. Even now...I don't use Instagram that much, but I've been dying to take pictures and post them."

"Why?"

"I guess just to prove that I was here. That I'm *doing* something. I know it's stupid. It's like a habit I'm trying to unlearn."

"I know what you mean," Violet said. "But good thing you are staying for two weeks, eh? So many people come out to places like this one for a weekend, maybe even less. They think it's like going into a bath and stepping out again. Like they can wash away all the dirt on their bodies and come out small and new again. It is not like that. It is like being burned in a fire and trying to grow your skin back again."

The reference to fire sent a wave of anxiety through Tessa's belly. "I came here because I was sad about everything dying," she admitted.

Laughter rang from the other side of the circle, distant-sounding. The mountains loomed to the north of them, their jagged outlines forming new pockets of night. Pressed-grape scent of wine, murmur of conversation. Black erasure between the stars.

"I came here because of a death also. My wife, she died last year. I've been going to these places ever since."

"Oh my god. I'm sorry." Tessa struggled for the right words, wanting to correct Violet's misconception. She hadn't meant actual human deaths. But she also felt the momentary urge to offer up the fact of her own loss—because she knew, without knowing how she knew, that Grise was dead. She had known this since the morning, since the first chirping of birds outside her window. Since the lightness had settled over her body.

But of course she said nothing about herself, and didn't bother to go back and elaborate on what she had meant, either. She stuck to the simplest, the most clichéd phrase in the book: "I'm so sorry for your loss."

"Don't be sorry," Violet replied, although her voice was light; she didn't seem to be judging Tessa's response at all. "She had a condition that shortened her life and caused her great pain a lot of the time. She lived much longer than anyone thought she would. I am mostly happy that I got to meet her at all." Violet's eyes crinkled as she smiled, the skin around them bunching like the bark of a tree. Just as Grise's skin, too, had been like the bark of a tree, although one much, much older. "And you know something strange, something wonderful? I think I can feel closer to her out here, in these spaces. Much closer than I did in the hospital, the place where she left me. There she was...not herself, not anymore. But here?" Her voice softened further, smoothing to velvet. "Here I feel almost like I can feel her, talk to her. I keep remembering things I forgot about—moments, memories from years ago, when we first met. Like her spirit is out here and it's giving them back to me, like she is saying, *Don't forget me. Here are the things we shared, long ago.*"

"That's amazing." Tessa had to swallow before she spoke again. "That's—that's beautiful." She remembered how her grandmother's face had appeared in her mind's eye when she woke up. How it had been utterly changed, finally free from the linear human experience. An image outside of time.

"It is how it is." Violet's tone was simple. She didn't sound overwhelmed or bowled over; she accepted this part of the natural experience as easily as most people accepted tax raises, bills, the slow inexorable shuffling from birth to death, those two points that made up the end and the beginning of everyone's line. But in the face of her grief, Violet was allowing herself to be moved backwards, to slide in reverse along the line, and she was laughing as she went.

Tessa saw it then in her mind's eye, as sharply as if she had searched for a picture of it: her ancient bristlecone pine tree, the gnarled structure that had come to represent, to her, life and nature itself. But now she could imagine it as something else. Her family's interconnected lives also formed a treelike structure, a massive trunk along which you could trace the existence of every one of her ancestors. Each ancestor formed a branch, and rather than enlarging, they shrank as they grew: the fullness of a child thinning out to a slender branch, lives scraped off to nothingness at their extremities.

But it was to nature that they all returned in the end. If you wanted to know the true history of someone, you had to look back and back, along the trunk. She thought she could see along it herself now, from where she stood at the newest, youngest branch of it: her own family tree, twisted with grief and loss and triumph and joy, her own Methuselah.

ACKNOWLEDGMENTS

Thank you to Stephen, Kate, and Ishmael for beta reading.

Thank you to my mom for her garden flowers, which I used in the cover.

Thank you to Nicholas for reading this before I even knew for sure what I was going to do with it. Thank you also to Samantha and Christine.

Thank you to Gary for all you do for me.

Thank you to my dog, Lily.

Amy DeBellis is the author of the novel *All Our Tomorrows* (CLASH Books, 2025). Her novella *The Widening Gyre* will be released from Lanternfish Press in 2026.

Her writing has been nominated multiple times for the Pushcart Prize and The Best of the Net, has appeared in the Wigleaf Top 50 Longlist, and can be found in *X-R-A-Y*, *Uncharted*, *Write or Die*, *Trampset*, *Fractured*, *Pithead Chapel*, *Vol. 1 Brooklyn*, and over 50 other literary journals.

Follow her journey on:

amydebellis.com
@amykatherrrine on Instagram
@amydebelliswrites on TikTok
@amykdebellis on X

9 798218 828257